IT SEEMED LIKE A COMPLIMENT TO ME

BY BRIAN DANIELS

IT SEEMED LIKE A COMPLIMENT TO ME

BY BRIAN DANIELS

ISLANDPORT  PRESS

ISLANDPORT  PRESS

Islandport Press
PO Box 10
Yarmouth, Maine 04096
www.islandportpress.com
books@islandportpress.com

ISBN: 978-1-934031-51-3
ISBN: 978-1-944762-02-5 (ebook)
Library of Congress Control Number: 2018942577

Islandport Press
P.O. Box 10
Yarmouth, Maine 04096
www.islandportpress.com
books@islandportpress.com

Publisher: Dean Lunt
Cover illustration by Teresa Lagrange, Islandport Press
Author photo by Kevin Bennett

Printed in the USA

To my children, Joe and Meghan
—two amazing human beings.
You make your Dad very proud.

CONTENTS

AUTHOR'S NOTE

On a refreshing autumn day in October 2008, a dozen or so of the people nearest and dearest to my heart invited me to take a seat in my own living room and proceeded to give me a good talking to. My daughter, Meghan, was, as usual, the first to speak. "Dad, you're a big old smart alec. You shouldn't say the things you do in a roomful of people. It's rude, and it's embarrassing. You're better than that!" As I scanned the faces of my family members and friends, it was clear she spoke for the clear majority.

So, being a thoughtful, caring husband, son, father, brother, and friend, I decided right then and there to respect their wishes. I would no longer blurt out thoughts like: "You don't need to lose any more weight, Eva. You look good with a little extra junk in the trunk." Although it seemed like a compliment to me, I rarely say such things anymore.

Now, I write them down instead. In 2008, I started writing a blog: *Thoughts of an Average Joe by Joe Wright*. Some of my friends asked me: "So why *by Joe Wright*? Why not by Brian Daniels?"

The answer is simple. Creating a (usually) lovable, fictitious character to reminisce about the good ole' days and to express concerns about life in the modern world gave me license to be even more ridiculous. Furthermore, if anyone is offended by Joe's rants, I quickly explain the offending remarks are his, not mine. Joe wouldn't hesitate to let you know: "You are just too damned sensitive and you need to lighten up and get over yourself."

In 2009, some newspapers started publishing Joe's commentaries in a column by the same name as my blog. So, I've been able—for the most part—to honor the request of my loved ones. I no longer blurt out offensive remarks in a roomful of people. I now write and publish those *Thoughts* for potentially millions to enjoy.

I was thrilled, in 2014, when my book, *Thoughts of an Average Joe*, was published by Dean Lunt and Islandport Press. As a result, many readers have come to know Average Joe Wright, a sometimes clueless, aging dude who loves to hunt and drink beers, but struggles to cope with growing old, understand his wife, and, in general, rages against the annoyances of the Twenty-First Century. Average Joe is an everyman that you might recognize.

I am blessed to have shared my life with many fascinating characters who have provided nearly endless fodder for Average Joe's stories. Many of these wonderful folks have read *Thoughts of an Average Joe* and point out that the stories are sometimes based on more fact than fiction. For sure, many of the tales in this book are *nearly true* as well.

In this follow-up to *Thoughts of an Average Joe*, our grumpy curmudgeon further familiarizes you with Smalltown through visits to the likes of the Kingdom County Fair, Jack Cafferty's Filling Station, and the Sunset Lanes Bowling Alley.

Joe is prone to bouts of nostalgia and how good things used to be. You'll also meet more Smalltown characters—characters you just might recognize from your own town—like crusty Davis Doppen, Aunt Eunice, and "Smalltown Playboy" Wilbur Pillsbury. Not to mention Joe's father Rufus Wright Jr., which will give you a little insight into how Average Joe came to be, well, Average Joe.

Average Joe isn't shy about letting you into his life. He wants you to know him and doesn't hesitate to admit that he sometimes lies, hates lousy service, and fears that he is becoming more and more like his father.

Many of the essays in *It Seemed Like a Compliment to Me* were originally stand-alone articles to appear in a newspaper or blog, but some have been altered, edited or combined for this book.

Joe is aware that he may be (then again, he may not be) the most opinionated guy in Smalltown and doesn't apologize. He's genuine, frank and unwavering. He'd tell you he's not mean, he's just sometimes misunderstood.

Average Joe makes me laugh. I hope you'll find his ramblings funny, too. If not, well, as Joe would be quick to point out, there must be something wrong with you.

SMALLTOWN

There's a reason my hometown is small—most folks don't want to live here.

Granted, some flatlanders from the cities and suburbs south of Smalltown drive up in July for the annual Bag Balm Udder Fun Fest, become enamored of the rolling green hills, pristine glacial lakes, and breathtaking views, and decide to flee the commotion of urban life to settle here in Kingdom County.

They rarely last a year.

For some reason, these well-meaning folks move here and immediately set about trying to make Smalltown more like the place they just fled. It doesn't take long before Rick London or Davis Doppen or another local tells them to pack up their Volvo, stuff it full of their big city ideas and haul it all back from whence they came.

Some claim there isn't much here in the way of culture and entertainment. I don't get it. I mean we may not have an opera house or an indoor movie theater, but we do have the Kingdom County Fair and the New Moon Drive-in Movie Theater, where just last week I saw the Kingdom County premier of *Ferris Bueller's Day Off.*

They (and by they, I mean those unidentified people that always seem to say stuff) say this is a hard place to make a living. I don't think that's true either. There are plenty of jobs here. A person can cut trees, raise dairy cattle, work at Small-Mart, fill those famous green cans with Bag Balm, or flip burgers at the Railway Café. And every forty years or so, the town doctor or lawyer retires, creating another shovel-ready job opportunity.

Granted, it can be hard to find a date with someone in Smalltown who isn't also clinging to a branch of your family tree, which I guess can discourage some young folks from staying here.

As I've said before, one wonderful thing about living in Smalltown is that everyone knows your name. One tough thing about living here is that—you guessed it—everyone knows your name. Margie Stewart, down at the Smalltown IGA, can even tell you how many Pabst Blue Ribbons I bought last year. (It's a lucky thing she's good at math, because it's a big number.)

It seems the southern folks who sail their cute Hobie Cats on Lake Willowbee in the summer and then decide to move here are a bit particular about their water. They don't like hard water—better known as ice. Once they realize the top layer of their beloved lake is three feet of hardness for seven months of the year, it leaves a bad taste in their mouths and they've headed back south before the geese return to Lake Willowbee.

The good news is that we saw a particularly tough winter this year. That should help keep Smalltown small—just the way I like it.

I REMEMBER WHEN WATER WAS FREE

When I was a kid growing up in Smalltown, if you'd have told me I'd someday be spending a buck and a half for a bottle of water, I'd have suggested you visit the state mental institution. Heck, my dad wouldn't even spend that for a six-pack of Narragansett.

And just the other day, I paid seventy-five cents for air to inflate the tires on my pick-up. Seventy-five cents for air. It made me think back to the days when I'd ride my Schwinn over to Jack Cafferty's Garage and fill up the tires. He had a bright red pumping station out by the street with a sign that read "Free Air." I remember, at the time, thinking, well, what other kind is there? Back then, I'd work for an hour stacking firewood for seventy-five cents. I'd be damned if I'd spend that hard-earned cash paying for *air*.

In the 1960s, Mom and Dad must have paid a little something for telephone service. But I can remember they didn't pay as much as the wealthier town families because we had a party-line—meaning a telephone line we shared with others, including Mrs. McManus, the busybody up the street, who could listen in on Mom's conversations with my Aunt Clara. However, we certainly didn't pay for television reception. It seemed magical to me, as a kid, that moving pictures and voices of *The Lone Ranger* or *The Ed Sullivan Show* just floated around in the air. All we had to do was turn the rabbit ear antennas just right and the black-and-white images would come to life on our Sears & Roebuck TV set. Sometimes, it was hard to tell the Lone Ranger from Tonto, but it was free.

Now, I pay ninety-five dollars a month to get 302 channels and, most of the time, I still can't find anything worth watching. In fact, I pay an additional fifteen bucks a month so I can rent black and white DVDs of *The Lone Ranger* and *The Ed Sullivan Show*.

Still, it's the water for which I most resent paying. I live in the country and have a drilled well, so most of my water is free. My friends in the village have "town water," which means they pay for the water they drink, and then pay again to flush it after they filter it through their kidneys.

When my daughter, Maggie, was a teenager she made pretty good money working as a waitress at The Loon's Cry, a restaurant that catered primarily to wealthy summer people. She once told me about a lady in fur and diamonds who rudely pushed away the ice water Maggie had poured and said, "Take this tap water away, young lady, and bring me some bottled water—French bottled water."

"Yes, Ma'am," Maggie replied and took away the lady's water glass. Two minutes later, Maggie returned to the pompous shrew with the same water in a fancier glass complete with a slice of lemon. Mrs. Hathaway sipped the "new" water and proclaimed, "Now that's delicious water. It's Perrier, isn't it?"

"Why, yes Ma'am, it certainly is. You have a very discriminating palate," my little darling replied.

"Well, I know good water."

In the end, everyone involved was happy. Mrs. Hathaway got her "French" water. My daughter's boss got two dollars for a glass of tap water, and Maggie got the satisfaction of serving just desserts to a pretentious woman, who thought herself better, and smarter than her little girl waitress from the back woods.

I suppose, some of the best things in life, like vindication, are still free.

WINTER DRIVING

Every time I drive during a blizzard, I can't help but wonder why so many idiots are out on the roads in such weather. Even a moron or a flatlander should know better than to risk his life—not to mention, most importantly, risking mine—by driving in a ton, or so, of death machine on shear ice or drifted snow. Don't people listen to that cute weather gal, Natalie, on Channel 3? For crying out loud, she went to a year of meteorology school and another three years of charm and beauty school. She ought to know what she's talking about when it comes to the science of weather. When she tells folks to stay off the road, she means *you*, Suzie Ski Bunny. Keep your all-wheel-drive Lexus home and right-side-up somewhere in Massachusetts.

I get a charge out of the fancy SUVs with down country license plates whizzing through Smalltown on their way to the Bull Mountain Ski Resort. These BMWs and Mercedes are decked out with studded, heavy-duty blizzard tires, a roll bar, and grill protector as if they were preparing to haul an 1,800-pound bull moose out of the Victory Bog swamplands or drive through a blizzard in the Alaskan tundra. In fact, they never have, and never will, leave the safety of highway or shopping mall asphalt.

These flatlanders think that four-wheel-drive means they can drive in any weather at any speed, which explains why I see so many $60,000 status symbols with their Michelins pointing toward Jesus and their owners wondering: *What just happened?*

My buddy Roy's wife, Mimi, *is* smart enough to know not to drive in stormy weather, but loves to shop. It's an obsession. A disease. She'll trek to the Kingdom County Mall in any weather. She'll drive her Chevy Trailblazer in a blizzard to buy the flowery curtains she so desperately needs for her kitchen (and then drive back the next day to return them and shop some more).

Roy and Mimi live on Island Lake in a town of the same name. Island Lake is a poor town since the paper company shuttered in the early 1970s. (Mimi hates it when I refer to her home as a poor town.)

Last year, a huge snow storm hit on Black Friday, but that did not deter Mimi from taking advantage of the big sales at the mall. Unfortunately, she didn't save any money.

She said she was headed to The Music Factory to buy me an Elvis double CD but when she "got to the crooked bridge at Bigsbee's Crossing and hit my brakes. The next thing I know, I'm spinnin' like a top and headin' for the snow bank."

Luckily, while she tore off the front bumper, she didn't get hurt. It did cost Roy $800 to fix her rig. And I never did get my Elvis CD.

It just goes to show you—folks should stay home when it's storming out. Sure, there are emergencies that require some of us to drive in such conditions—like a one-day special on Bud Light 30-packs down at Dan's Market, or, of course, if the new *Uncle Hank's Trading Post* happens to hit the store shelves on the day of a blizzard.

YOU JUST DON'T STEAL FROM THE SMALLTOWN IGA

When I was a teenager, Dad owned the Smalltown IGA store. That meant, like it or not, I had a job for the next ten years.

In any village, the local grocery store is not only a place to pick up Pabst Blue Ribbon and a box of Slim Jims on your way to or from work—it is also a community social center. Many folks just hang out near the checkout counter for gossip and company.

Smalltown IGA was one of those stores with an outdoor display of fruits during the four months when temperatures stayed above freezing. The stacks of peaches, pears, plums, and apples were quaint and attractive, but a pain for my brother, Sam, and me. Each night, we had to lug all the fruit inside at closing time and then lug it all back out the next morning. That kind of effort made young Joe tired.

In the summertime, guys like Nuckie Leonard (260 pounds of wiggle) and Alphonse Lebrecque would stand outside the store, smoke (I'd walk a mile for a Camel), eat fresh cherries, and spit the cherry pits onto the sidewalk alongside their cigarette butts. Mind you, they never paid for the fruit, and cherries were pricey.

My old man was a kind and easy-going man (the apple doesn't fall far from the tree), and would joke with them about paying for the cherries, but they weren't bright enough to catch on.

One warm July evening, Dad decided it was time to make his point a little more forcefully. Dad was a friend of the town cop, Louie DeChaines, and called him for a favor. I was working the checkout as Louie pulled up to the storefront, blue lights flashing and siren blaring. He jumped out of his cruiser—as quickly as a big man can jump—and handcuffed and arrested Nuckie and Alphonse for "approximately 100 counts of theft by consumption, and littering of a public sidewalk."

Nuckie nearly choked on a cherry pit and the look on his face was priceless. Alphonse was too stupid to know what was happening.

"But . . . but . . . but they're just cherries," Nuckie protested. "We've done this every night for two months."

"Exactly, big man," Louie explained. "These cherries are for sale. You've been shoplifting."

"Jim," Nuckie yelled to Dad. "Tell him we weren't stealin'."

Dad just grinned as the thieves were squeezed into the back seat of the police cruiser. Dad never pressed charges, but Nuckie and Alphonse never ate another of Dad's cherries.

Usually my father was more subtle with shoplifters.

Vanilla extract comes in small bottles and is about fifty percent alcohol. It was a popular item for low-life shoplifters who needed a buzz, but didn't want to work a job to pay for it.

Pete Jackson was one of those losers, and Dad knew it. The last time Pete stopped into the IGA, he roamed the store and eventually stepped up to the checkout to pay for a pack of Juicy Fruit gum.

"That'll be $10.20," Dad said.

"$10.20?" Pete replied. "For a freakin' pack of Juicy Fruit?"

"It's twenty cents for the gum, and ten bucks for stolen merchandise."

Dad slammed the cash register receipt on the counter for dramatic effect (The old man watched a lot of John Wayne movies).

"You can pay now and never step foot in this store again, or I can call Officer DeChaines."

Pete placed a sawbuck and a quarter in Dad's massive hand and sheepishly left. He never returned.

Dad was also a man of integrity. Once Beth Willis, a Smalltown Elementary School teacher, was purchasing two pounds of peaches for a cobbler. Beth is a little woman—about four-foot-ten—but is quite buxom.

She placed a half-dozen freestones on the scale and gasped.

"Wow," she exclaimed. "I can't believe six peaches weigh four pounds."

Dad glanced over to see Beth on tip-toes trying to read the scale. "Beth," he said quietly. "Your left one is on the scale."

Beth, a good sport, stepped back and howled. "Oh, a pound- and-a-half. That's more like it."

She paid Dad and thanked him for not taking advantage of her.

"Oh Beth, I'd never cheat you. What kind of a boob would do a thing like that?"

THE WEST HAVEN FIELD DAY

While Smalltown is not big, it is the largest town in the area and is surrounded by towns and villages too small to host events like the Kingdom County Fair or the Bag Balm Udder Fun Fest. These communities do, however, like to host a get together each summer and so, for as long as I can remember, they've each organized their own town field day.

A field day is a refreshing blast from the past. A wholesome, family and community-oriented day of parades, horse pulling, horseshoe throwing, chicken barbeque, and craft sale. It's kind of like a county fair, but without the carnies and noisy rides.

Dub Kaler was a character I remember from my childhood growing up in Smalltown. He was a little man with lots of energy and spoke rapidly in a language all his own.

Dub drove a cattle truck for the local slaughterhouse and picked up old cows and bull calves from local dairy farmers and transported them to the slaughter house to be transformed into T-bone steaks and ground chuck.

"Git, git, git you 'ole girl," he'd say as he slapped an old Holstein on the backside. "Git up dat wamp and inta dat twuck afor I turn ya inta gwound humbugga wight hee-yah an now."

Dub liked his job, and on the weekends, he enjoyed playing horseshoes. He was pretty good and took home the West Haven Field Day Horseshoe Tournament trophy a few times. But not in 1977. That year, he was runner-up. To add insult to injury, he lost to a woman, Jane Easterbrooks.

Jane was a rugged girl about half Dub's age and twice his size and for some reason she took a shine to the old cattle prodder. She could throw a shoe, but knew Dub was a little better, so she'd got inside his complicated little head to defeat him.

"Good luck honey," Jane teased. "You play your cards right and you can take me home as a trophy."

"De onliest twophy I'm takin' home is dat one ovah day-uh, ya son ub a biscuit," he sputtered pointing to the tall golden trophy he coveted.

"We'll see about that, sweet cheeks. I think you're gonna lose to a girl this year."

The crowd of men hooted and hollered. "Dub, you gonna let that sweet thing take the trophy from ya?"

"No, I ain't dammit. No way, not in my wifetime, dod-dammit."

The match was a close one. Tied six times before the final shoes were thrown. It was 20-19. Dub needed just one point to claim the prize. He threw two shoes close enough to score a point each. Jane's first shoe landed a foot short of the pin.

"You've had da waddish now, Janie. Wooks wike dat twophy's goin' home wid ole Dub again."

Jane's final shoe seemed to float in slow motion as it turned one revolution in the air and landed on the pin with a metallic clang—a game winning ringer.

"Dod-dammit," Dub yelled. "Dat was pure wuck. I want a weematch."

Jane laughed. "I tell you what, two shoes each. You win, you take the trophy home. I win, you take me for a spin around the dance floor at the fiddle contest."

"Yer on."

Jane threw first and her shoe landed beyond the pit. Her second shoe landed a bit short. She failed to score.

"Watch 'em an weep," Dub taunted.

His first shoe missed well to the left of the pin. His second shoe appeared headed for the pin but fell just short and bounced off Jane's shoe, pushing it into scoring range and then bounced out of the pit.

"Looks like I win two trophies today."

She threw the golden prize over one shoulder, Dub over the other, and headed for the dance floor.

She rested her metal trophy on the stage and muckled onto Dub like a Pit Bull on a Porterhouse as the fiddler broke into the Tennessee Waltz.

She held him close—really close; his eyes bulged and spectators swore they heard cracking ribs.

THE GEEZERNASIUM

Winnie and I sometimes take the grandkids to the park to play on the swing set, slides, and jungle gym. They seem to like that, but I find all the other screaming kids annoying. Why can't they all behave like Hanson, Sumner, Gracie and Ella? And why don't they just get out of the way when my perfect grandkids want a turn on the slide or swings?

Last week, I had to kick a little girl off the swing set. She thought that just because she was cute, with her little blonde ringlets and big blue eyes, she could hog the swing for minutes on end. Well, I had to remind her that I'm old and needed a place to sit. Kids these days can be so inconsiderate.

That experience got me to thinking that Smalltown should open an adults-only outdoor playground. We could call it the Geezernasium and restrict it to folks over forty.

I don't want to be relaxing on the swing set and have a bunch of screaming kids running around. I also don't want to listen to some twenty-somethings saying: "Oh my God," "like," or "awesome" ad nauseam.

The Geezernasium would be cool—and easy. The swings would be powered by electricity, no pumping required, and there'd be some hammock swings. It'd be nice to have a giant screen TV in front of the swings so I could enjoy the Red Sox or watch reruns of *Duck Dynasty* while enjoying the ride.

The slides would be gigantic and offer a gentle, relaxing downhill glide following the escalator ride to the top. No stairs—I just got my new knees and don't want to wear them out.

A full cocktail bar with mixed drinks and ice cold Bud Light would be great and maybe a pharmacy in case I forget my inhaler.

There'd be a disc jockey playing only the good stuff from the sixties and early seventies—no disco, rap, heavy metal, grunge, or hip-hop.

Cell phones would be collected at the gate. If I'm enjoying a relaxing swing ride I don't want some dude next to me ruining it by loudly wheeling and dealing on his phone, checking his email, or texting non-stop. And I definitely don't want to hear Amy Amadon sharing the status of her Facebook friends: "OMG, Brenda is drinking like a cup of coffee right now. That is like awesome."

That's not awesome, Amy. The Grand Canyon is awesome. Brenda drinking coffee isn't even interesting.

Of course, all the rules in the world can't control Mother Nature.

It would be a bummer if an unexpected thunderstorm popped-up to ruin my fun at the Geezernasium. Maybe I'll just install a power hammock and a mini-fridge in front of the big TV in my living room.

SMALLTOWN TRAFFIC

My daughter, Maggie, lives near Beantown these days so, when we visit her, Winnie, my wife, and I must drive down to Boston.

There are too many cars in the city. Traffic is terrible. I can't believe people sit nearly still for hours driving from their overpriced homes in the suburbs to their jobs downtown.

I'm not sure why traffic gets so tied up. They seem to have plenty of roads. I could solve ninety percent of their traffic congestion with one word of advice—"Go!"

If folks just drove instead of stopping to gawk at every fender-bender or slowing to check their text messages, traffic would move right along.

Just "Go!"

It's that simple.

We don't have much trouble with traffic back-ups in Smalltown. Things move right along because drivers just go.

There is the occasional animal in the road. Elmer Barrington's oxen sometimes bust through the wire fence and hang out on upper Main Street. They're a load to move if they don't want to. They can be kind of ornery. I guess I might be a bit cranky too. Do you know how a bull becomes an ox? Yup, no question that could make one ornery.

On the outskirts of town there's a sign which reads: DEER CROSSING—231 COLLISIONS. There really are more, but the sign hasn't been updated since 2009. It would be an expensive proposition to change the sign every time a whitetail collides with a Prius. I'm not sure why they are keeping score anyway. Harriet Bingham, who is number than a pounded thumb, suggested at the annual Town Meeting last March that the town move its "Deer Crossing" to a place where there isn't so much traffic. True story.

One of the worst traffic jams in Smalltown occurred in September 1981. Reggie Coulombe stopped at the blinking red light on Station Street and then didn't budge. For nearly thirty minutes, drivers politely waited behind him for a spell before pulling out to go around him. At times, the backup reached as many as five or six cars.

Finally, the town cop, Howard Smith, finished his coffee at Raymond's Drug Store and walked over to see what was wrong.

Reggie was broken down alright, but it was him, not his car. Reggie was deader than a doornail (I guess there are degrees of deadness).

Apparently, Reggie was feeling poorly, shifted his Ford Pinto into Park and suffered a massive heart attack right there at the blinking red light, which has been known locally as Reggie's Light ever since.

Folks around town still talk about the Big Traffic Jam of 1981. It was a huge deal. Reggie nearly brought Smalltown commerce to a standstill that day. All because he could no longer follow my simple advice and just "Go!"

COWSPEAK

Winnie grew up on a dairy farm on the outskirts of Smalltown. Her brother, Rick, and his family still operate the farm.

Over many years of visiting the farm as an in-law, I've come to realize that farmers grow attached to their animals. In fact, I recall one Sunday dinner at which my nephew commented: "I like Doreen."

"Who's Doreen?" I asked.

My mother-in-law, Bea, replied: "Doreen is dinner. She was old and a little tough, but she makes a good pot roast, don't ya think, Joe?"

"Ummm, delicious," I replied as I choked down a chewy morsel of Doreen.

I often thought those cows had a pretty good life (for a while anyway) and wondered, if they could speak to each other, what they would say.

They must hear their owners refer to them as "dumb cows" from time to time. And admittedly, they do come across as less than brilliant.

I can imagine Jolene and Bertha, (cows seem to have old fashioned names—never Meghan or Desirae), in adjacent stanchions discussing their daily routine.

"Jolene, I'm starting to get hungry. Must be almost time for Kassie to bring us some oats. I like oats, don't you?"

"I do Bertha, and I like these long winters here in Smalltown when we eat inside all the time and don't have to go outside, walk around, and graze on grass. It's kinda like room service."

Sure enough, within minutes, Kassie delivers breakfast.

"That poor Kassie," Jolene says, her mouth full of oats. "She's awful thin. Probably from running around taking care of us. She just never stops."

"I know," Bertha replies. "She finishes feeding all of us and then she turns right around and hoes out all the cow flops and wet sawdust we make."

"Yup, and then she spreads new sawdust so we can start our busy day of moving oats and hay from one end of us to the other again."

Bertha finishes her oats and still feels hungry.

"I wish Kassie would get here with the hay pretty soon."

"Here she comes," Jolene reassures her friend. "Poor skinny woman. I'm not sure what Rick sees in her. I know he likes the chubby ones."

"Yes he does, doesn't he?" Bertha chimes in. "He calls me 'beautiful fat cow'."

"Yeah, me too. Or sometimes 'sweet fat thing'."

"I hope he gets here soon. My bag of milk is almost dragging on the floor and it hurts some."

"He'll be right along Bertha. At least I hope it's him. He has gentle hands."

"Yeah Jolene, he sure does. But that boy of his, Bert, is a little rough, and always in a big hurry."

Jolene snickers. "Kinda reminds me of that young bull, Leroy."

"Oh Jolene, you naughty cow. Leroy *is* always in a hurry, isn't he?" Bertha laughed.

"Yup, like he has something better to do. And you're right, that Bert is always in a rush, too."

Bertha burped.

"Yesterday, Bert was tugging on me like he was ringing the bell at Notre Dame Cathedral, so I smacked him upside the head with my tail . . . twice. 'Dumb cow' he calls me."

"That's funny, Bertha. They deliver our meals, clean our poop, make our beds and massage our udders. 'Dumb cows' indeed."

FESTIVAL SEASON

Summertime in Northern New England is the season for outdoor festivals and field days.

Many festivals celebrate a particular genre of music. The North Woods Blues Fest features about twenty artists performing hundreds of songs to the same melody using the same three chords. Each song is about a mean old woman (or man) who either ran off with the singer's best friend or ruined his/her life by getting run over by a freight train— driving the singer to drink copious amounts of moonshine or Wild Turkey and constantly whine and moan.

The Kingdom County Bluegrass Festival features the musical genre created by the likes of Bill Monroe and Flatt and Scruggs. It is essentially blues with a banjo. The whining and moaning is performed with a high lonesome sound usually sung with a southern drawl (even if the singer has never ventured south of Vermont), and is always sung through the nose.

Jazz festivals, like the one held every year up along the Piscataquis River in Northern Maine, showcase the music of artists like Miles Davis and John Coltrane. The songs seem to be short on lyrics and long—waaaaay too long—on improvised instrumental breaks. The musicians, apparently affected by dementia or copious amounts of moonshine, seem to forget how to end each song, which, consequently, can seemingly drag on for several hours.

There are festivals across the north country to celebrate the harvest of every kind of berry—blueberries, strawberries, raspberries, blackberries, and so on. None of these berry bashes is very exciting, but they all feature pies, cobblers and whipped cream—a few of my favorite things.

There are lots of festivals for foodies. There's a Clam Festival, Maple Fest, the Lobster Festival, and Cheddar Cheese Days. It's no wonder I'm fat.

Some festivals honor a young lady by crowning her the Strawberry Queen or the Poppy Princess. If I were a seventeen-year-old girl, I'm not sure I'd vie for the honor of being crowned Miss Holstein Heifer or participate in the Passumsic Pig Pageant.

Many little towns produce a product of which they are proud.

Lisbon Falls, Maine throws an annual Moxie Festival featuring that well-known soft drink which is seemingly made from coal tar, molasses, turpentine, and mud. Those who like it rightfully claim it is an acquired taste.

Smalltown is famous (alright, so maybe not *that* famous), for producing Bag Balm. Needless to say, there is a Bag Balm Udder Fun Fest every August. It is my favorite event of the year. What could be more fun than watching my grandkids run around trying to get a grip on a Bag Balm-covered, squealing, little porker? Now, that's entertainment!

And who wouldn't volunteer to judge the Softest Udder Contest? Smalltown is home to some of the smoothest teats in America and Bag Balm makes it all possible.

For me, though, the highlight of every Bag Balm Festival is the annual contest for the Dairy Association Golden Bag Trophy awarded for the most creative use of the golden salve. I'm a two-time winner of this esteemed prize. I'd have won again last year for treating that red, raw, chafed area I developed during that really hot spell we had in the summer of 2012, but the festival organizers couldn't find a judge willing to look under my BVDs to compare the Bag Balm treated side to the non-treated side.

FILL 'ER UP

When I was growing up in Smalltown, there were two gas stations—Blake's Esso and Jack Cafferty's filling station. They were weird little businesses. They did two things—they pumped gas and fixed cars.

These gas stations didn't sell beer, Slim Jims, or mocha cappuccino. They sold gasoline, engine oil, and fan belts. Oh, there were vending machines filled with R.C. Cola, Baby Ruth bars, and cigarettes, but there were no grocery stores attached, just a garage. They didn't even sell air. They gave it away! No wonder they are no longer in business.

There was no such thing as self-service gas pumps in those days. Nope, folks pulled their giant Chrysler or Chevy up to the pump and drove over a small black tube that sent a "ding-ding, ding-ding" signal to Jack inside the garage. Jack crawled out from under Ethel Sanderson's Ford Fairmont and sauntered over to the driver's side window

"Two bucks, regular, please," you would tell him.

"You got it," Jack cheerfully replied. He'd then pump several gallons of Amoco's finest into the eight-miles-per-gallon beast, clean the glass, check the oil, top off the radiator, and slap a new inspection sticker on the windshield.

Of course, all that service came at a price. Jack charged twenty-five cents a gallon for the fuel. It took a little of the sting out of the price, though when Dad brought home a free dinner plate or coffee cup after each fill-up.

Part of the reason there was no "self-service" is that there were no credit cards. That is not to say there was no credit. If a man was short on cash and needed gasoline or a new alternator, Jack would have him sign his name to an oil-stained cash register slip and collect later.

21

Sometimes that didn't work out so well for Jack, but in a small town, there was usually a way to make things right. If the customer didn't have firewood, maple syrup, or a trailer load of cow manure that Jack could take in trade, he usually shamed him into paying by using the Smalltown gossip mill. One "accidental" slip of the tongue to Ethel Braley about a deadbeat customer and the words spread across town faster than flame at a gasoline spill.

Jack did have trouble collecting from Reggie Rideout once, though. Reggie had charged up a sizable amount for an oil change and some gas back in 1966 and was making no effort to reduce his debt.

Reggie was the town's only lawyer and had fallen on hard times because no one in Smalltown was divorcing and the new town cop, Howard Smith, was following folks home from Luigi's lounge to ensure their safety rather than arresting them for drunk driving. It seems Reggie was pretty good at lawyering but didn't know an oil filter from a dipstick.

One hot morning in July, Reggie pulled his 1963 Dodge Dart up to Jack's gas pump and asked for three dollars worth of regular. Jack pumped the gas, popped the hood, checked the oil, and slammed it shut again. Rideout signed the gas receipt and turned the key to his Dodge.

"My car won't start," Reggie complained as engine sputtered and whined.

"Thirty-five dollars and sixty-seven cents will make this old Dart run like a champ," Jack grinned.

"I don't have that kind of cash on me."

"You can park your car right here until you do," Jack offered. "Only two bucks a day."

"Well, you cheap old bugger," Reggie sputtered as he stormed off in the direction of the Smalltown Savings and Loan around the corner.

Twenty minutes later, Jack slid $35.67 into his oil covered Made-Well pants, popped the hood of the Dodge, and replaced three spark plug wires.

"She'll start slicker'n snot on a glass door knob now," Jack announced.

Sure enough, the little Dart fired right up, and Reggie left rubber half way down Station Street.

NEARLY TRUE HUNTING STORIES

I just returned from a week at the Smalltown Boys' hunting camp up near Island Lake. I've been going there for deer season most of my life as have my old man, brothers and, brothers-in-law.

Naturally, over forty-some years we've made some memories. The stories we repeat year after year, are mostly true—what my buddy Barney calls "no-kidders" (or something like that)—but I've noticed the stories change with each passing season so I decided I'd write some of them down because, at the current rate of growth, some of the deer taken will exceed 600 pounds during my lifetime.

K.C. once killed two partridge with a single 30-30 bullet. That's a "no kidder." Dad pointed out a fat grouse strutting under the game pole and challenged my brother to bag it with his rifle. K.C. fired and, sure enough, the bird toppled over. Upon retrieving his trophy, he found he'd killed two birds with one shot. There wasn't enough meat for a complete meal, which is a shame because partridge breast tastes just like frog legs.

And then there was the time K.C. hunted for hours trying to flush a bird or two and couldn't scare up even one. He was sitting deject-edly on the tailgate of his Toyota Tacoma—he pouts when he doesn't have success hunting—when the damnedest thing happened. A large hawk—obviously a better hunter than my brother—flew right at K.C. and his truck, flapping his wings for all he was worth, but having diffi-culty gaining altitude because of the heavy prey in his talons. Apparently realizing he'd crash into K.C. if he'd continued at the same trajectory, the big bird dropped his prize at my brother's feet and flew off.

My brother-in-law, Jimbo, once killed a ten-point buck with his knife. He was hunting over by Hawk Rock when a massive buck jumped from its bed and ran up the ridge to avoid Jimbo. Granted, I've seen many creatures avoid Jimbo. After one display of his dance moves up at the Bull Mountain Lodge, the young women would pair up or make a beeline for the exits at the sound of the first few notes of "Shout" or "Hammer Time".

On that cold November morning, my brother-in-law pulled up his 30-06 and fired, dropping the ten pointer in his very large tracks. Later, we discovered no hole in the giant deer, only a crease in his skull between the two antlers. Jimbo had knocked the buck out cold—like he'd delivered a Mike Tyson sucker punch—and then had officially killed the deer while removing its vitals with his knife.

Jimbo is a good hunter. He scouts before the season starts to get a better idea of what the deer are up to and, I'm guessing, to get some time away from my sister, Vanessa, who is a sweet person—like me— but maintains a big honey-do list.

I'm not one to argue with success or to work any harder than need be, so I, for years, would follow Jimbo through the woods sometimes "accidentally" sitting practically underneath the tree stand he was occupying. Why reinvent the wheel?

Once Jimbo caught on to my wicked plan, he walking miles into the wilderness, figuring I was too lazy to tail him that far from the warmth, food, booze, and poker table at camp.

He was absolutely right.

As it works out, Jimbo's "leave lazy Joe behind" strategy corresponded in time to the advent of mobile phones as a way to communicate in the woods. My brother-in-law still kills some big deer, but now he kills them miles from camp. It is an uncanny coincidence that every time he calls for deer-dragging assistance, my cell phone service is non-existent.

THE SMALLTOWN WINTER OLYMPICS

Smalltown, of course, will never host the Winter Olympics. Every January, though, we celebrate the season of Jack Frost with The Smalltown Winter Carnival. It's quite an event and one of the area's annual social highpoints.

Like the Olympics, our Winter Carnival kicks off with a torch lighting. Our torch is much more modest, however. It is actually a citronella fueled tiki torch like the ones we light by the summer campfire while the mosquitoes eat us alive. For some reason, at 10 degrees below zero, it seems the citronella is much more effective at repelling those buzzing, flying, bloodsucking pests.

The contests of the Smalltown Winter Carnival are a lot different than those of the true Olympians. In 1984, skiing events were discontinued because swishing under the influence of Schlitz was deemed too dangerous.

Snowmobile drag races are held on Lily Pond to add the excitement of a potential splash during the January thaw. Usually, the Smalltown Fire Department succeeds in saving the drivers who end up in the drink. If not, well, I've heard that's nature's way of culling the herd.

There's no luge track at the Smalltown Outing Club. In lieu of luge, participants race down a snowy hill on gigantic tractor tire inner tubes (old, patched up tubes donated by farmers Rick London and Tom Simpson after they are deemed inadequate to handle the load of a John Deere or Massey Ferguson). One of them also proved inadequate to support the weight of Big Martha McKay and exploded, propelling Martha to the finish line for the gold medal and causing a minor avalanche.

Instead of a four-man bobsled, Smalltown races canoes down the ski slope. In 1997, me and the boys who play in the Basic Bluegrass Band took home the gold. It is amazing how fast 1,100 pounds of overweight bluegrass musicians can travel in an Old Town Tripper on ice while playing Dueling Banjos, the *Deliverance* theme.

One of the highlights of the carnival is the Snow Sculpture Contest. Last year, my buddy, Roy, and some fellow *Baywatch* enthusiasts, made a waist up sculpture of the show's most famous blonde bombshell which, when they finished, actually did look a lot like her. Unfortunately, we got a thaw that week and by the time of the judging, their sculpture looked more like Anderson Cooper than Pamela Anderson.

CHANGING LIGHT BULBS

Light bulbs changed while I was busy making a living, raising rug rats, chasing whitetails, and fishing for smallmouth bass.

The little woman sent me down to Small-Mart last Saturday to buy a package of bulbs to fit the living room table lamps. You know, the classy kind that show silhouettes of deer, bear, and moose when the light is on.

When I got to the lighting aisle in the store, I was shocked to see there were about a hundred yards dedicated to light bulbs. My head was spinning at all the choices. Eventually, I found a Small-Mart employee who wasn't "on break" and asked for help.

Trevor, as it said on his blue name tag, looked about fifteen and had enough piercings and metal hardware to conduct electricity, so I thought he might be the perfect "associate" to help me with my light bulb questions.

"Trevor, I need some sixty-watt light bulbs," I said.

"What kind?' he asked.

"What kind? The kind that, when I turn on the lamp, I can read my *Uncle Hank's Trading Post* to see if anyone is selling a used toilet for cheap."

"Well, there's CFL, LED, tungsten, halogen, fluorescent, or incandescent," Trevor replied.

"I want the regular kind. You know the kind Thomas Edison invented about 120 years ago."

"Oh, did you know him, sir?" Trevor asked.

"Very funny, Trevor." I was wishing he was older so I could rearrange the fishing tackle on his face.

"You want incandescent then. You sure you don't want to switch to CFLs?"

Trevor showed me a compact fluorescent lamp. It was shaped like a pig's tail.

"That don't look right. Why would I want that?"

"It uses a lot less electricity and lasts longer. You'd want a 13 watt."

"No pea brain, I told you I need a 60-watt bulb. With 13 watts, I won't be able to see squat, even with the little woman's reading glasses."

"Sir, a 13-watt CFL gives off just as much light as a 60-watt incandescent. Let me show you." Trevor turned on a floor model lamp.

"That ain't bright enough," I grumbled. "No way that's the same as a 60 watt."

Finally, after thirty seconds, the bulb got brighter, maybe equivalent to the 60-watt bulb I'm used to.

"So Trev, you say these last longer. How often will I throw one in the trash can?"

"Oh, you won't."

"What?"

"What?"

Trevor shook his metal-laden head.

"The CFLs contain mercury, so you can't throw them in the regular trash. You have to take them to a disposal center."

"Okay, that does it. I'll take a regular bulb."

"What shape?" Trevor asked.

"What shape?" I repeated. "Light bulb shape."

"Well sir, we have the A-line, the flame shape, the round candelabra . . ."

"I want the regular shape, you know, the one that looks like Grammy Wright from behind, when she bends over to weed her dahlias."

"Okay then, the A-line. Flicker or flame?"

"What?" I yelled, my frustration mounting.

"Some folks want a bulb that flickers or looks like a flame. It's kinda sexy."

"I don't need sexy. Winnie and I like it dark when we're sexy."

"Would you like a three-way?"

"A three-way? Excuse me?"

"No, no, sir. I mean, do you want a bulb that gets brighter or dimmer depending on how many times you turn the switch?" Trevor turned a little green. "So what kind of socket do you have?"

I whacked my own head. "A light socket, dammit," I screamed.

"Well, now there are C7, T10, A15, GU10, G24 . . . "

"I just want the same old base I've been using for fifty years!"

"Alrighty then." Trevor rolled his eyes. "A medium base."

"Exactly."

"So, you want a Warm Light, Cool Light, Soft White, Bright White, Red, Yellow, Green, Blue, Purple . . ."

"Aaaaaaahhhh," I yelled. I can't take any more. I stormed out of Small-Mart and headed to Fred's to get some candles.

I marched to the front and asked the clerk where I could find candles.

"Scented or unscented," she asked.

THE KINGDOM COUNTY FAIR

In some towns, I suppose it's the annual Sailboat Regatta and Lobster Bake at the yacht club or the Tea Tasting and Soprano Diva Festival down at the opera house, but the social highpoint of the year in Smalltown is the Kingdom County Fair. Kids save their nickels and dimes all year for rides, games, cotton candy, and the greased pig catching event. Grownups stuff ten dollar bills into weekly budget envelopes labeled "Beer Money–Fair."

The Fair—pronounced with two syllables (Fay yuh)—is a celebration for the senses. The smells, flavors, sights, and sounds of the fair can send a person into sensory overload.

Walking around the agricultural area fills the nose with a pungent bouquet of hay, silage, and animal sweat with a fine manure finish. Of course, the finish changes drastically as one moves from the chicken coop to the cow barn; the horse paddock to the pig pen, etc. Truth be told, I prefer the essence of horse pucky to that of chicken scat. But significantly more pleasant are the aromas found on the midway. It's hard to imagine nose candy more pleasing than the midway's blend of pizza, French fries, cotton candy, hot dogs, and grilled sausages with onions and peppers. It's no wonder you find so many large people at the fair. I often wonder if many of them were actually thin when they first pulled into the fairgrounds parking lot.

I love fair food. The ladies of the Smalltown Methodist Church always have a food booth and offer some hearty homemade entrees. I have to admit though, I tend to patronize the carnival vendors and opt for the grease-drenched dough boy smothered with powdered sugar. I can eat healthy at home, although I rarely do. They say you are what you eat, so no wonder I am starting to resemble the Pillsbury Doughboy.

The fair is noisy. The sounds of the midway resemble those of a bizarre, drug-induced nightmare like you see in the movies. There are screaming kids on the Tilt-a-Whirl, and the creaking, clanging, music-blaring Scrambler, the crashing of bumper cars and the rat-a-tat pitch of barking carnival workers—"Three balls for a dollah, win the little lady a teddy bear." It's all enough to make a guy drink beer.

In the old days there were even what they actually called "girlie shows." Carnie barkers tried to entice men to pony up some money and step inside a tent to see scantily clad "beautiful dancing girls," although I suspect they more often found a peroxide blonde roller derby queen with bad teeth and lots of cheap tattoos. "She shows it all. She's hotter than a cowboy's pistol on the 4th of July . . . "

There's still a lot to see at the Kingdom County Fair. I like to visit the agricultural exhibit halls to see the gigantic pumpkins, check out the blue ribbon winning zucchini and find out who grew the potato that most resembles Elvis. That's all quite a contrast to the flashing lights, bright colors, and shiny rides of the midway.

The Kingdom County Fair has always been a real boon for many local businesses, not the least of which was Dad's store, The Small-town IGA. We sold beer—LOTS OF BEER—during fair week. We sold lots of other stuff, too—wine, potato chips, Fritos, Devil Dogs, Twinkies, cigars, and cigarettes—you know, the staples for a healthy, wholesome lifestyle.

Every customer at the store would talk about the fair. Claude Campton was the pastor of the Smalltown Congregational Church. His son, Alex was a friend of mine. Reverend Campton was a comical minister and loved to talk. I remember one year he shared his fair experience with me as I rang up his Spam and Velveeta.

"Joey, I told Alex not to go into the 'girlie show' or he'd see something in there he shouldn't see. Of course, he went in anyway and I was right. He saw me."

I guess everyone has their favorite part of the fair experience. Mom likes the Bingo booth, Uncle Jack likes the horse racing, Winnie enjoys the exhibit halls, and Dad spends most of his time at the horse pulling. As for me, I'm torn between the pig scramble and the grilled sausage subs and I like that the former ensures a nearly endless supply for the latter.

I MISS THE BARBERSHOP

Smalltown lost its only barbershop about a decade ago when old man Whitney dropped dead right in the middle of giving my Uncle Herbert his monthly flat-top.

Roland Whitney was old. He was the only barber I ever saw for a haircut until I was pushing fifty. While I was growing up, Dad would take my brothers and me to Roland's Barbershop every six weeks, or so, for a buzz cut. I always enjoyed the experience.

I liked sitting in the big chair which Mr. Whitney would pump up with his right foot to bring me to his height. I couldn't tell, because he always wore the same baggy blue pants, but I always figured Roland's right leg must be twice the size of his left.

As a kid, I liked the big mirror I faced while in the barber chair. These days, I'd rather look at a Holstein's backside than spend twenty minutes staring at my own face. I'm sure some would argue that there isn't much difference except that there isn't as much bull crap coming out of the Holstein.

Old Mr. Whitney was a talker. Once in his chair, you were his captive audience and he'd run his pie hole non-stop. He'd go on about the Red Sox and how they fell apart in September; he'd rave about the New York Giants (that was before the Patriots were New England's team), and tell the same old stories every haircut.

My brothers and I would giggle because on the ride to the barbershop we'd imitate Mr. Whitney telling us how he could have been a professional baseball player if he hadn't been drafted to fight in Korea.

"Did I ever tell you I was a pretty decent second baseman in my younger days?"

Snicker, snicker—I tried not to look at my brothers in the mirror.

"Yup, played for the Montpelier Senators. Semi-pro. Mighta been drafted by the Red Sox but had to go fight in Korea."

"Hee, hee . . . huh, huh." My face was the color of Dad's hunting hat from trying to suppress laughter.

"Oh, this razor tickles, don't it Joey?"

"Yup." Finally, I could laugh out loud along with Sam and K.C.

"Don't laugh at your brother, boys. You're next," Mr. Whitney would say.

As I got older, I still enjoyed my haircuts. It was the same old stories and, basically, the same haircut, but I found it relaxing and grew to understand why Dad always fell asleep during his trim. I'd wake up, though, when the warm shave cream hit my face. It felt great, but, by then, I knew old man Whitney drank a lot and the thought of him with a straight razor to my neck made me pucker a little.

Nobody stepped up to fill Mr. Whitney's shoes after he died. I guess men don't want to stand for eight hours a day and shave the hair from the ears of crotchety old geezers like me.

So, these days I go to see Tammi down at the Shear Pleasure Beauty Shop where the little woman and her friends gets their hair cut and roots colored.

It's not the same.

First off, the waiting area is often full of blue-haired old ladies and *Good Housekeeping* magazines—not an *Outdoor Life* or *Hot Rod* magazine to be found.

The place smells funny, too—all lavender, roses and weird smells from strong chemicals. It's enough to make your hair curl!

And then there's Tammi. She's pretty and friendly enough, but she doesn't know squat about the Red Sox, Patriots, or the breeding habits of whitetail deer. She uses scissors, not electric shears, and rambles incessantly about some desperate housewives in New Jersey or that cute little dress she bought on sale at Small-Mart.

To add insult to injury, I pay twice as much for Tammi to cut my hair even though I seem to have misplaced about half the hair that once covered my noggin.

I guess that old red, white, and blue barber pole has gone the way of telephone booths and full service gas stations. But, oh, how I long to hear about Roland Whitney's baseball career.

HOW DID WE SURVIVE CHILDHOOD?

We spent a lot of time outdoors when I was a kid. There were too many of us to stay inside. It would have driven our parents crazy. Plus, there were no video games to play, one or two fuzzy channels on the black and white TV, and we couldn't tie up the phone for hours talking to our friends because we shared a "party line" with two or three nosy neighbors. We played in the dirt, made forts in the dirt, and ate a fair amount of dirt. We didn't seem to get sick from it and I don't remember friends having allergies.

My three-year-old grandson, Hanson, was sent home from preschool one day last month with a reprimand for endangering the health and welfare of his classmates. His teacher found contraband in his Spongebob Squarepants lunch box—a highly dangerous Fluffernutter sandwich. His parents—my son, Jake and his wife, Jenna—have been shunned by other Learning Land parents ever since.

Somehow my brothers and sisters and I survived riding in cars and trucks without seatbelts. There were six of us and sometimes we crawled around the back seat or the front seat or even sat on Dad's lap while he drove through town. (That ended, though, when my sister, Kelli, peed on Dad as he drove us all to church.) I can even remember riding in the bed of Uncle Jack's pickup truck with the family beagle, two sisters, a bicycle, a bear carcass and a dozen, or more, empty beer bottles. Somehow we all survived.

These days, we are all protected, to some degree, from second-hand smoke. Folks can't smoke in stores or restaurants or even bar rooms. That wasn't the case when I was a kid. Growing up in Smalltown, if I was with adults, I was in a room or a vehicle full of tobacco fumes, although Dr. Braley would sometimes remove the cigar from his mouth while listening to my polluted young lungs with his cold stethoscope.

We didn't know the sun's rays were bad for us either. There was no SPF 50 sunscreen. Heck we slathered on baby oil to enhance the sun's skin destroying potential. We were living in the North Country. It was a short summer and we needed to burn and burn fast. It hasn't killed me yet, though I've had a few ugly lumps lopped off my back.

I was an active kid; I played sports and rode my Schwinn Stingray like I was Evel Knievel—the faster, the better. I never wore a helmet.

Skiing was dangerous back then, too. There were no safety bindings on the skis and nobody wore headgear other than a warm hat we called a tuke. I lost control once on a double black diamond trail and took on a small poplar tree with my head. Thank God, because I could have broken an arm and missed beaver trapping season.

I certainly didn't wear a helmet to ride my bicycle. To do so would have guaranteed a beating by the cool guys which would have resulted in head injury far greater than any I sustained from the crashes I endured while learning to do wheelies down Eastern Street.

Protecting our kids is a good thing. But it just seems to me we get a little carried away with it these days. Besides, it's the damage done to my body during my carefree childhood, that made me the wrinkled-up, wheezing, cranky guy I am today. Who would want to miss that?

HUNTING CAMP CLUTTER

I grew up on Eastern Street in an apartment upstairs over my Mom's parents.

My Memére was a hefty woman and she gave great hugs. Pepére used to say that she gained so much weight out of shame. After a full meal, she'd pick at the leftovers and say: "It's a shame to waste these two strips of bacon," or "It's a shame to throw out this one slice of chocolate cream pie."

Our hunting camp, up near the town of Island Lake, is cluttered for the same reason. It seems as though anytime my folks or my brothers or sisters or I replace something in our homes—because the old one is broken, worn out or ugly—we take the replaced item up to camp.

"It's a shame to throw this twenty-five-year-old recliner away. It doesn't recline anymore, and it leans to the right a bit, but a little duct tape will keep the rest of the stuffing from falling out. Let's take it to camp."

My brother, K.C., and I did an inventory at camp last week. The following is a *partial* list of the junk we've accumulated over the past five or so decades.

We have forty-two coffee cups: twelve still have handles, but of those twelve, seven have chips on the rim. I've cut my lip twice drinking coffee at camp.

We cook on an old gas stove up there. Two of the three burners work, but you have to ignite each with a match or a lighter. We have thirteen lighters, including two shaped like rifles and one like a fire-breathing duck. Only two lighters actually make a flame, but we keep them all—just in case we need a spark someday.

It's difficult to move around in the living room. There are two mismatched sofas, both with broken springs. There are three recliners, two of which once adorned my Uncle Jack's TV room at his home. When new, their beige fabric matched. Now, they are each so stained with beer, Jack Daniel's, ketchup, and salsa, you'd never know they were once a pair. It's rumored that Uncle Jack fell asleep and peed on one of the couches after drinking too much beer on Super Bowl Sunday. We pretend we don't know that story.

There are dozens of dust-covered knick-knacks covering every flat surface in the cabin. We've got porcelain bears, deer, moose, hula girls, dogs, cats, a three-legged cow and a one-armed Curt Schilling booblehead.

We're well stocked with salt and pepper shakers. There is a pair of dachshunds, the same white Tupperware pair you see in every hunting camp, two wooden figures with yellowed chef hats and a single frog pepper shaker. (His mate died in a beer salting incident in 1966.) We use only the disposable pair you can buy at any grocery store.

I found six decks of playing cards. Three decks of 51 cards—I'm not sure which cards were missing but they all had women in underwear on one side which is why Ol' Dad insists on keeping them. The one full deck is missing a corner on the Ace of Spades.

There are seventeen pens at camp. None of them write.

I counted fifty-six ball caps in our home away from home. They advertise such things as Red Man chewing tobacco, Smalltown IGA, the Island Lake Dance Hall, and Pabst Blue Ribbon beer. We'd have more, but we ran out of nails to pound into the walls as hat hangers.

We've got two TVs, one stacked atop the other. Neither works since we live in a digital-only world these days. The bottom TV hasn't worked since Uncle D.I. poked a hole through the screen with his .22 revolver during the 1986 World Series just moments after the ball rolled between Bill Buckner's legs. It would be a shame to take it to the dump.

THE SMALLTOWN PLAYBOY

Wilbur Pillsbury is about my age and has always fancied himself God's gift to women.

Standing five-foot-three and dressing out at 205 pounds, Wilbur cuts quite a figure. He's thick around the middle, but narrow in the shoulders, giving him the look of a Weeble, which seems to make sense because when he's been into the Old Milwaukee, he wobbles, but for some reason he doesn't fall down.

The Smalltown Playboy likes to dress for the ladies. Luckily, he stockpiled a closet full of polyester leisure suits before they went out of style in the 1970s. He has a wide-lapelled suit—and a satin paisley shirt to match—for every day of the week, but for Saturday nights at Mo's Dance Hall, it's the powder blue number and the shiny, white patent leather shoes that make the cut.

Unlike many of us, Wilbur has never gone bald. Nope, he just parts his hair barely above his left ear and *swooooops* eighteen-inch-long tresses forward and then over his right ear and around to the back of his head. He then sprays his jet-black locks with about a half can of Breck Super Hold hairspray, giving himself a poor man's Donald Trump look that will hold up to a category five hurricane.

Our ladies' man knows there's more to being a sex symbol than just appearance, which is why, on Saturday nights, he leaves his AMC Gremlin in the driveway and takes his mother's Ford Pinto to the dance hall. After all, if that Pinto was good enough to take Becky Patoine to the Senior Prom in 1970, it is still good enough to get the job done today.

Not only does Wilbur work hard to look the part of a playboy with his clothing choices, but he has developed some impressive moves on the dance floor, too. The house band is never more than three notes into "Johnny B. Goode" before Wilbur storms the hardwood. His footwork repertoire plays out like a revue of every dance craze to grace *Dick Clark's American Bandstand* from 1962 until the middle of the disco era, which I'm guessing is about the time his mother's antenna broke, making it impossible for Wilbur to watch Channel 8.

During a five-minute rendition of the Chuck Berry classic, Wilber will transition clumsily from The Pony to The Jerk to the Twist to The Swim and, for his grand finale, mimics a disco-era John Travolta doing The Hustle—although a sawed-off, overweight, spastic version. Wilbur knows a lot of dance routines, there is no doubt. Having watched him though, I can't help but wonder what music he is really hearing in his head.

I once overheard Wilbur explaining to Sylvia Charrette—talking slowly trying to emulate Clint Eastwood in a Dirty Harry, "Go ahead punk, make my day" style—that women love him because he knows all their *erroneous* zones. I'm certain Sylvia didn't ask him for proof.

Annie LaCroix is one of the most beautiful women in all of Kingdom County and is also extremely kind. So, one hot August night, when the band at Mo's kicked off "Johnny B. Goode," she accepted Wilbur's invitation to "boogie." In a show of solidarity, three of Annie's girl-friends joined her as our playboy twisted, spun, gyrated, and hustled his way around the dance floor.

After the final "*Go Johnny go. Go, go, go,*" Wilbur strutted off the floor, puffed up like a Tom turkey in heat.

"Whoa Wilbur," I said. "What's your secret?"

"That's simple, Joe," he replied. "I got more *testestrogen* than most guys."

DAVIS DOPPEN WAS A CRUSTY OLD BIRD

Growing up a grocer's son in a small village wasn't always "all that and a bag of IGA chips." My older brother, Sam, and I logged a lot of hours at the checkout counter, including shifts on Christmas Eve and New Year's Day morning. It did, however, allow us to meet some interesting characters.

We tried to have fun with our friends at the Smalltown IGA and gave many of them secret nicknames. Thelma, the "Old Duke Lady," would slip a pint of cheap wine into her purse, wait for the checkout line to disappear, and then walk up to the cashier, open her purse to show the bottle (as if we didn't know), and pay us the $1.09 for the vintage classic.

Percy, "the smelly cat rancher," would show up every Friday evening for twenty-five pounds of Kibbles and Bits Ocean Medley and three bags of cat litter. The litter was apparently not that effective. It was Percy, not the thirty cats, who was "smelly."

Ephus, the eighty-seven-year-old "Glue Sniffer" was always happy. He hadn't worked on a pair of shoes since Small-Mart started selling foreign-made penny loafers for $3.99, but he went to his cobbler shop daily. He said it was the "high" point of his day.

My favorite regular though, was Davis Doppen, a crusty, old farmer of Dutch descent whose mission in life seemed to be to give me a hard time.

Davis was a tall man with reddish-blonde hair and bad teeth. He always carried with him the essence of wood smoke and bad breath. Every Monday, Wednesday, and Friday he'd shuffle into the store with a scowl on his face. I'd always greet him with an over-the-top, "Good morning Mr. Doppen; how are you this fine day?"

"Ummph," he'd grunt as he made a slow-motion sprint for the walk-in beer cooler.

His purchase was always the same—a case of Black Label beer and six packs of Pall Malls (which he pronounced "Pell Mells").

After a year, or so, of ringing up his order, I asked Davis, just for fun: "What do you do with all this Black Label?"

"What the hell kinda stupid question is that?" he fired back. "I drink it. What the hell do you think I do with it, numbskull, (I'm cleaning this up to keep it PG-13), wash my face?" (Again, I'm keeping it clean.)

That was the beginning of a game we played for years. I'd ask a stupid question and he'd reply with a crusty retort.

On bitter cold days, I would ask, "Cold enough for ya Mr. Doppen?"

"No, Peabrain, I'm sweating like a hen haulin' logs. Course it's cold enough for me. You must lay awake nights thinkin' of numbskull questions."

I did. It was fun.

Old Davis had but one speed, so one July day he limped in to find shelter from the driving rain of a pop-up thunder shower and was dripping from his hat to his Wolverines.

"Is it raining, Mr. Doppen?' I chided.

"Gawd no, it's a %$#^& gorgeous day. But the bridge was out, so I swum 'cross the river. Gotta rush home so I can put up the %$#^& hay while the sun's shining."

About once a week, Davis would also show up with two little toe headed boys—his grandsons Barnie and Byron—following him. The youngsters, about five and seven years old, would bypass the candy counter and head right for the cigar rack where they'd each grab a single William Penn Corona and bring it to the checkout to add to their grandpa's pile of healthful purchases.

After witnessing this behavior for a couple years, I was truly curious.

"What do those little guys do with the cigars?" I asked.

"They smoke 'em ya fool. What the hell else would they do with 'em?"

It's funny how life works out sometimes. Years after Dad sold the IGA, I married a lovely lady with reddish-blonde hair who liked to drink beer. Yes, Winnie is Davis Doppen's granddaughter.

At Thanksgiving dinner in 1982, with the whole family gathered for turkey and all the fixings, Grandpa Doppen asked, "Joe, I've been wondering; how'd an ugly mutt like you end up with such cute young 'uns?"

"I had my way with your cute granddaughter, you crusty, old buzzard. Thanks for asking."

THE GALS AT WORK

The office at the company where I work has women answering phones, dispatching trucks, handling the bookkeeping, and telling old guys—like me—what to do.

One of them, Brittany, is a twenty-something and let's just say is a lot more concerned with the color of her toenails than the national deficit.

One day last month I was delivering a load of gravel to Jake Jenkins up in Island Lake when Brittany called me on the CB radio to tell me Jake was at the construction site waiting for me. She could hear my CD playing in the dump truck.

"What's that you're listening to?" she asked.

"Tex Ritter," I answered.

"I never heard of Tex Ritter."

"He goes back a few years. He was a country and western singer."

"Oh, one of those wicked old country singers like Kenny Chesney?"

"Yeah, like Kenny Chesney, only older. He was John Ritter's father."

"I never heard of John Ritter either. Is he a country singer, too?"

"No, he was an actor. You know him. *Three's Company?*"

"Oh Mr. Wright, you're naughty. Mostly I think two's company and three's a crowd, Although, you know, sometimes three's fun, but I didn't know you old people knew about threesomes."

Candi, who works in payroll, is very attractive, especially for Smalltown, and for years she was the frequent target of the flirtations and sometimes inappropriate comments from stupid young men. As a result, she developed a sharp tongue to reduce a would-be lady killer to a verbally neutered knucklehead to anyone else within earshot.

Just last week, Hank Masure asked Candi what it would take to get her into the back seat of his Silverado King Cab. Without batting an eye, she told him: "There isn't enough whiskey in Lynchburg to make that happen."

Another day Luke Stetson asked what it would cost him for a lap dance to which Candi replied: "I don't know, Luke. What is the going rate for plastic surgery, gym membership, two years of Weight Watchers meetings, and a personality make-over?"

I'm too old and too smart to flirt with Candi, but that doesn't mean I'm immune to her razor-like tongue.

When I told her I'd be taking a week off in November to hunt whitetails in Maine, she asked me how many deer I'd shot in my lifetime.

"Oh, more than I can count," I lied.

"Wow," she replied. "Good for you and I bet, as a young man, you bagged a few dinosaurs, too."

THE WRIGHT FAMILY VACATION

My old man, Rufus Ralph Wright Jr., is a frugal man—a cheap bugger. But he loved Old Orchard Beach, Maine. He claimed he liked the pier and the sandy beach, but I'm fairly sure it was the Canadian women in their skimpy bikinis that were the attraction. (Definitely *not* the Quebec men in their skimpy Speedos.) So, every three years or so, when I was a kid, Dad would sell some beaver pelts, cash in a boatload of Ballantine Ale quart bottles he'd emptied, and book us a week at the beach. Usually, his brother, Uncle Bing, would tag along because he, too, was ready for a break from the same old Smalltown scenery.

The beach at Old Orchard is a pristine, white sand paradise. Everything else there in the 1960s was downright tacky and we loved it.

For that one week we had a change of menu from Mom's hearty standards like red flannel hash and venison stew. Mom's meals were always delicious, but you know what they say about variety. On our Old Orchard vacations, we sustained ourselves on pizza, fried dough, French fries, and cotton candy. It was great!

Dad says that Old Orchard was once an exclusive resort with fancy hotels and restaurants. The wealthy folks from Boston and New York would ride the train north and spend most of the summer there. My how things had changed.

In the sixties, Old Orchard had a carnival feel to it. An amusement park sat right on the beach and there was no escaping the clanging and hissing of rides like the Tilt-O-Whirl and the Scrambler or the screams of their riders.

For the Wright family, visiting Old Orchard was like visiting a foreign resort. It seemed like nearly all the tourists at Old Orchard were from Quebec.

As I've mentioned, Dad and Uncle Bing seemed to enjoy the Canadian women in their string bikinis even though, at least in my mind, most of those French-speaking ladies were over fifty and some of those bikini-clad ladies must have been pushing 70 with skin the color and texture of dark leather (or Naugahyde), which covered flabby arms that flapped in the breeze like the Canadian flag flying over the Bienvenue Motel.

The men from north of our border were, of course, just as tan and flabby, but wore even less. They'd squeeze 250 pounds into a bathing suit the size of a small sling shot. I once overheard my dad telling my uncle that, to make things worse, some of them would try to enhance their sex appeal by stuffing a potato down the front of their Speedo.

"No way," said Uncle Bing.

As it turned out, the next day was the Fourth of July and Uncle Bing showed up at the beach wearing a red, white and blue Speedo—and a carefully placed potato.

Our full body shivers at the sight of it all turned into full body laughter when Uncle Bing emerged from the frigid waters of the North Atlantic no longer with a bulge in the front of his swimsuit, but a lump in the back. An ocean wave caused his Yukon Gold to shift positions.

I have fond memories of our beach vacations and, to this day, I can't eat a potato without . . . well . . . actually, I've given up potatoes altogether.

MY GRANDSON, SUMNER, IS A WILDMAN

My second grandson, Sumner Wright, is a stocky little guy. He's kinda chubby, kinda bald, likes to eat and drink and is frequently getting himself into trouble. He's a one-year-old version of me!

I've told you about his older brother, Hanson, who is also a corker. Like many brothers, it seems that these two couldn't be more different from one another.

While Sumner will eat anything that lands within his reach—hot dogs, chicken, steak, ants, grasshoppers, milk, beer (oops), ice cream, chips, cake, popsicles, dirt, crackers, cheddar, gouda, Limburger or Alpo—his brother couldn't care less about food. Hanson loves milk; hates food. Offer him a hamburger and you'd think it was pork liver. Chocolate pudding? It might as well be blood pudding. Broccoli? He'd rather have a tooth pulled.

As a result, Hanson is a bit small for his age and Sumner is a bruiser—a bruiser just biding his time. You see, Hanson, being a typical three-and-a-half-year-old big brother, likes to push his little brother over or tackle him for no reason. Sumner seems to take it well. He just rolls with the punches, for now, and gives Hanson that "you just wait" grin.

Hanson is a fairly careful kid; he tends to avoid trouble. He doesn't like "boo-boos" and isn't too crazy about getting dirty either. Sumner, on the other hand, is always in search of danger.

Sumner reminds me of Popeye and Olive Oyl's baby, Sweet Pea, who was always crawling across four lanes of speeding traffic, barely avoiding being squashed by a dump truck or fire engine. He'd also creep along steel girders and fall off the end of an I-beam 200 feet above the ground, but always land on another beam being moved by a giant crane at just the right moment to avoid crashing to the earth below.

Sumner is a plump, but stealthy mischief-maker. If there is a toilet within toddling distance, he'll find it, reach in, and splash around like a warbler in a bird bath. An unprotected electric outlet is considered a challenge: "Why won't my finger or Mommy's pen fit in here? I see big people sticking things in here all the time."

The little woman has some big houseplants. Sumner loves to climb onto the large pots that contain them and pull out little handfuls of dirt. Once he reminds himself that potting soil looks like chocolate but tastes like . . . well . . . dirt, he throws it onto the floor where it contrasts nicely with the white shag carpet we've kept since back when it was in style in the seventies.

And then there was the time someone gave my littlest buddy a pretty red Christmas ball to play with. Within seconds, his lips, tongue and half his face were covered in bright, red dye. He looked like a round, little baby clown. Luckily, a quick call to poison control got his Grampa Wright off the hook.

My grandson, Sumner, is indeed a little wild man, but I like that he has an adventurous side. It may get him into some trouble over the years to come, but he'll have some fun and he can rest assured his Grampa Wright will be there for him, wherever his adventures take him . . . the hospital . . . the carnival . . . the Kingdom County Jail.

PLAYING MUSIC FOR THE OLD FOLKS

Walt, Munzie, Barney, Roy, and I have been playing music together, as Basic Bluegrass for more than twenty years. We often play for the senior citizens at the Pine Hill Nursing Home and Assisted Living Center. It's a great place to play because the audience seems to appreciate us. I think maybe we sound best to those who don't hear well. Furthermore, as we approach "The Golden Years" ourselves, we sometimes repeat a song verse because we can't remember the words to the verse we should be singing. It works out well at the nursing home because they don't remember they just heard that same verse just a few moments earlier.

We don't typically get paid to play for the old folks, so if we mess up, oh well, it's good practice time. And Lord knows we need practice. Besides, we're not so many years from being on the receiving end of the entertainment, so we think of nursing home gigs as "paying it forward."

Something we've noticed, over the years, is that the Pine Hill residents like to hear songs from their youth.

In the late 1990s, they wanted to hear Hank Williams songs. Munzie learned "There's a Tear in My Beer" and sang it with feeling, I think because he was going through female companionship with the speed of the Energizer Bunny.

That audience grew up with Big Band music. There were five of us, each over 200 pounds, so we sort of qualified as a "big" band. Bluegrass music is known for that "High Lonesome Sound," so we thought we'd learn an Andrews Sisters song. You haven't lived until you've heard "Boogie Woogie Bugle Boy of Company D" done with a banjo and mandolin. Pine Hill banned us from playing that number because, at the annual Valentine's Day party, several residents were inspired to jitterbug which resulted in two broken hips and a minor heart attack.

By 2010, the old folks wanted to hear everything from George Jones to disco music. "White Lightning" wasn't much of a stretch for a bluegrass band and Walt and Munzie do a great job on "Dueling Banjos," but we struggled a bit to sound like the Bee Gees. It was worth the effort to hit those high notes in "Stayin' Alive" though to see Linwood Haywood (dressed in the powder blue, way-too-tight leisure suit he was married in), do the Hustle with his harem of oxygenarial, I mean octogen . . . eighty-something-year-old widows.

As I look ahead to my nursing home years, it makes me giggle to think of some young band of sixty-something-year-old whippersnappers coming by to play "Stairway to Heaven" and "Jumpin' Jack Flash."

I'm just hoping I look better than Mick Jagger and Keith Richards do now.

MY COUSIN, JANINE, SAYS THE DARNDEST THINGS

I wish you could meet my cousin, Janine. Those of you lucky enough to know her will attest that she is a one-of-a-kind character who resides in a place called "Janine's World," where no one else lives or has ever visited. Janine isn't stupid by any means or measure. She just doesn't think like the rest of us. Let me share a few examples.

A few years ago, some friends and family came over to help Winnie and I erect a stockade fence in the back yard. By the end of the day, we were some tired, achy, middle-aged fence builders. Winnie complained about her sciatica. Our buddy, Barney, was hobbling around on sore knees and complaining that the Seagram's Seven wasn't easing the pain or making him walk any better. My brother, K.C., whined about his shoulders and said he thought a massage would feel good, but insisted he wouldn't go back to the Smalltown Gun Shop and Health Spa because the last time he did that the therapist rubbed him the wrong way.

"They do have hot tubs down there though. Maybe we should pool our money and rent one," he suggested.

Janine chimed in.

"That's a dumb idea, K.C. By the time we bring it here, fill it up with water, and wait for it to get hot, it'll be midnight.

My cousin doesn't fully understand modern technology. Her son, Durwood, is not bright, but he can operate a smart phone as if he studied at the Massachusetts Institute of Technology.

Janine invited us over for a cookout last year on the Fourth of July. It was some hot and humid that day and we were all sitting on the porch sweating and complaining. Durwood whipped out his iPhone, pushed a few buttons and announced: "The Weather Channel says it's 92 degrees here."

Janine wiped her brow and said: "It sure feels hotter than that, Durwood. Take your phone out in the sun and see what it says."

Janine's favorite TV show is "The Following." Her husband, Ullrick, says he got home from working the night shift at Smalltown Tool and Die and there sat Janine in front of the TV looking quite perplexed.

"What's the matter?" Ullrick asked his wife.

"It's so weird," she said. I'm watching "The Following" but it's all different. The story is different, the actors are all different, and the characters are all different. It's like a different show altogether."

"Well maybe the football game ran a little late and you *are* watching a different show."

"Nope. This is "The Following." The announcer said so at the beginning."

"Are you sure?"

"Yes, I'm not an idiot. Just before the show started, they said: 'The Following may contain violence and adult situations.'"

DON'T SEND ME POSTCARDS

This past January, while I was out in the sleet and freezing rain, shoveling a three foot drift of heavy snow left at the end of my driveway by the town plow guy, the mailman delivered four credit card applications, the *Victoria's Secret* catalog, and a postcard from my sister, Vanessa.

It seems Vanessa and her husband, Jimbo, were vacationing in Cancun. The photo on the postcard was of a pristine beach with palm trees swaying in the gentle tropical breeze as the sun set over the Gulf of Mexico. It looked like Heaven on Earth and made me want to strangle someone.

On the back, Vanessa wrote: "Having a wonderful time. Wish you were here. Love, Vanessa and Jimbo"

Errrrrrhhhhh!

Why do people send postcards like that? Don't they realize it is just rubbing it in that they are in Paradise while I'm home freezing my butt off and breaking my back shoveling snow?

It wouldn't be so hard to take if they'd be honest and tell me the whole story of their vacation. They never send a card depicting an airport security line two miles long with the inscription:

"Stranded at O'Hare for two days, lost our luggage, and feel violated after the TSA cavity search. You're lucky you stayed home. Love, Jimbo."

And I've never received a postcard depicting a Mexican hospital on the back of which read:

"Having a terrible trip. Jimbo drank the water and suffers from Montezuma's Revenge. Hasn't left the toilet for two days. Love, Vanessa."

Oh no, it's always some picture of "paradise" with a description of the delightful time they are having while I'm suffering at home.

So, if you are my friend or relative, and you really care about me, go on vacation if you want to, have a good time if you must, but let's make a deal.

Don't send me a pretty postcard and get the little woman all up in my face about never taking her to nice places. In return, I won't send you one from my vacation "upta camp."

My postcard, by the way, would show a photo I took last deer season of Uncle Herbert in the outhouse looking all hung over, dehydrated, and constipated, his eyes bulging like a tree frog's from trying to force the issue. On the back I'd write a cute little note: "Uncle Herbert needs an enema. Wish you were here. Love, Joe"

MY AUNT EUNICE IS A RIG

Aunt Eunice, my mother's older sister, doesn't fight as much since she moved to the Northeast Senior Center. She's lived there for the past three years because: "I want to help take care of the old people."

Aunt Eunice is eighty-six.

My aunt is a character; my understanding is that she always has been. She's tough, rough around the edges, and says what's on her mind. She talks fast, swears like a pirate, and is sometimes a bit hard to understand.

"I'll get to you bombah" (by and by), she'd bark at a waiting customer. "You just shut up and wait yer $#*&@# turn."

Aunt Eunice never married. I don't think she could find a man as tough as she was. She ran the bark stripper down at Eastman's Sawmill for forty years.

Junior Reynolds had a crush on Auntie and tried, in his own awkward way, to flirt with her as he'd drop off a load of hemlock at Eastman's.

"I wouldn't want anyone else to strip for me," he said with a grin that exposed all four of his teeth.

"Shut your damned pie hole, Junior, and drop yer logs ovah theyah," Aunt Eunice said. "And you bettah save up some money 'cause, with that face, the only way yer gonna get a woman to take her #$*@ing clothes off is to pay to get inta the girlie show upta the county fair."

Forrest Boisvert asked Aunt Eunice to lunch one day. "You hungry Eunice?" he asked.

"Libit (a little bit)," she replied.

"How 'bout I buy you a burger over to the Railway Café?" Forrest offered.

"I can buy my own damned burger, dipstick. And I'd rathah eat it by myself than to hafta look at yer ugly #@&$ing mug while I'm tryin' to swallow it."

I'm not sure why Aunt Eunice never married. I guess some men are just too thin skinned.

Aunt Eunice was, for the most part, a loner, but she liked to drink Budweiser and when she drank Budweiser, she liked to dance . . . and fight.

On Saturday nights, you could usually find her at Mo's drinking beer and dragging other women's husbands onto the dance floor where she'd shimmy and shake to "Bubba Shot the Jukebox" or "The Watermelon Crawl." Inevitably, before the night was over, a jealous wife would confront her.

Betty Maynard, for one, didn't care for Aunt Eunice bumping and grinding like a pole dancer after pulling Rusty Maynard onto the dance floor.

"You're drunk Eunice," she said.

"Of course I'm drunk, Betty. Why else would I dance with your ugly #ss loserball husband?"

For some reason, Betty took offense, slapped Auntie, and was rewarded with a bloody nose.

Rusty rushed to his wife's defense and, as a result, couldn't open his left eye for a week.

I love my Aunt Eunice; she's a lot of fun. All of my aunts were wonderful and I could count on most of them for cookies and cocoa. Aunt Eunice was good for Budweiser and Beer Nuts.

NUCKIE LEONARD

There's a committee that actually tries to get people from away to visit Kingdom County. Some say that tourists are unpleasant, like a bacteria that causes those unsightly, puss-filled, red, painful pimples and boils. I agree they can be very annoying, but I am told we need them. I say the jury is still out on that one.

In 2005, the Kingdom County Tourism Committee decided to build a trail system through the beautiful hills, fields, and forests of our homeland in an effort to attract people from places like New York City, Boston and Philadelphia to come visit us and spend a butt load of money.

As a result—from May through foliage season—the streets of Small-town are now just loaded with BMWs, Mercedes, Cadillacs and other expensive four-wheel-drive vehicles, most of which have never touched tires to anything but asphalt. Attached to these expensive rigs are several fancy bicycles each of which, I'm guessing, are worth more than my Dodge Ram pickup truck.

Nuckie Leonard, like Roy and me, is a regular at the Railway Café. On Saturday mornings, during the hot months, the place is just boiling over with tourists in stretchy, black short pants and skin-tight, colorful shirts.

Nuckie took a shine to the fancy bike outfits and, unfortunately, found one on eBay that almost fits him. Nuck looks like he might be the offspring of the Michelin Man and the Pillsbury Dough Boy's daughter. He's about 320 pounds of Jell-O. Under no condition should he wear Spandex or Lycra, which leave nothing to the imagination. Now, I never imagined that Nuckie was hiding the body of an

Olympic swimmer under his old overalls, but, at least, I could ignore the image of that body. But you pack all that Jell-O into a Spandex suit and it's like a car wreck; you don't want to look, but you can't help yourself. And once that image is in your memory bank, there's no erasing it. It haunts you for life.

They say that black, tight-fitting material is slimming, but on a truly fat person, the compressed flab has to go somewhere. It doesn't disappear, it just gets displaced. In Nuckie's case, the result is a massive muffin top and jelly fish kneecaps. It ain't pretty. All of that so he can enjoy improved aerodynamics as he rides his 1978 Schwinn with the fat tires, chrome fenders and twin, rear newspaper baskets the two blocks from his place to the Café for his daily hot chocolate and a six-pack of donuts.

MY OLD MAN HAS A WAY WITH WORDS

My old man says stuff most of us have never even thought of. Unfortunately, most of the things he comes up with are colorful—too colorful to share with the pious, straight-laced, God-fearing folks that follow *Thoughts of an Average Joe* . . . or even the other ninety-seven percent of my readers.

Yup, Dad has a way with words. If you say something that rubs him the wrong way, he won't rebuff you with something as generic as: "Bite me." He'll tell you to: "Kiss my (backside)."

If you ask most folks what size Timberlands they wear, they'll answer with a number like 8 ½ or 11. Not the old man. He's likely to say: "I wear a 9 but 9 ½ feels so good that I buy a 10."

I once told Dad I was going to hunt near the Lost Nation Road on the opening day of deer season. Dad knows the woods around Smalltown better than most and wanted to tell me that there were very few deer down there. Do you think he said: "Joe, don't bother huntin' there. It's a waste of your time."? No, instead he told me: "Joe, you might as well fart in your hat and sniff it as to hunt by the Lost Nation Road."

My father has a way of sharing words of wisdom that makes those words memorable.

He once defended Gladys Toothaker, the homeliest woman in the greater Smalltown area. He overheard the morning gossip club down at the Miss Smalltown Diner describing Gladys as "a two-faced old biddy."

Dad couldn't help himself. He lifted his chair and plopped himself right down there among the old hens and said: "Gladys ain't two-faced. If she was, she sure as hell wouldn't be wearin' the one she's got."

My grandparents—Dad's folks—were quite poor when he was a kid. The old man has a favorite story to describe his childhood.

"My folks didn't have a pot to piss in when I was growing up. At Christmas, Mom wanted to get me somethin' I needed. Pops wanted to get me somethin' to play with. So, Mom made me a pair of britches and Pops cut holes in the pockets."

The old man has many such "words of wisdom" he's shared over the years. I suspect many of them he learned from my Grampa Wright. Sometimes though, Ol' Dad is just quick-witted.

At my sixtieth birthday party, I was concerned that Dad was getting too much sun and asked him he wanted to move to a shadier spot. When he declined, my buddy Barney—a stocky guy—stood between the old man and the sun and said: "I'll provide shade for ya Jim."

Ol' Dad, in the blink of an eye, replied: "Yeah Barney, you'll provide enough shade for me and three or four of my friends."

GLADYS HARTWELL KINNEY, MY AUNT'S "BEST FRIEND"

Gladys Kinney died last week. She lived down the street from our family most of her life.

I was visiting my Aunt Phyllis as she read Gladys's obituary in the *Smalltown News*.

"Gladys wrote her own obit," Aunt Phyllis said.

"What makes you say that?" I asked.

"She lied about her age right to the grave," Auntie exclaimed. "It says here she was born in 1928. I was born in 1930 and she's a good five years older than I am."

"Hmmm," I replied.

"Sweet mother of Jesus. It says she married Harold Kinney in 1946."

"So?"

"So, she shacked up with Harold from 1946 until November 1948. She married him about four months before her first daughter, Ethel, was born. Her daddy, Tank Hartwell, was a big, mean man and, with it being deer season and all, his 30-06 was handy."

My aunt reported that the obituary went on to mention Harold and Gladys's four kids, Ethel, Earlene, Kenny (yup, Kenny Kinney), and Darla.

"It don't mention that Kenny was born around 10 months after Harold left to fight in Korea and looks a whole lot like his best friend, Ferland Jones."

"My lovin' Lord, I can't believe what I'm readin' here," Aunt Phyllis shrieked. "Says Gladys was a proud and patriotic American and a dedicated member of the Veterans of Foreign War Auxiliary."

"She was in the Auxiliary, Auntie."

"Only 'cause she liked to hang out at the VFW hall where they had a bar and a couple of those one-armed bandit gamblin' machines. I hear she liked to guzzle down those cheap Sombreros."

I had no comment.

"Jesus, Mary and Joseph. Says here she is survived by her four children, ten grandchildren and four great grandchildren."

"Yeah, that sounds about right," I replied.

"Yup, but also it goes on to say she is also survived by her best friend, Mavis Masure."

"So?"

"So, that's a bunch of horse pucky. Nobody was ever a more devoted friend to Gladys Kinney than I was."

MY GRANDDAUGHTER, GRACIE, IS SPECIAL

My granddaughter, Gracie, is brilliant. I know every grandparent thinks their grandkids are future Rhodes Scholars, but this is different. I'm not seeing Gracie through the eyes of an adoring grandfather. I'm just telling it like it is.

I've seen what love can do to a grandfather's judgment. Why just last week I was talking to Wilbur Jenkins, who works at Dan's Market, about how smart Gracie is and he said: "I know what you mean, Joe; kids these days are so advanced. My grandson, Wilbur the third—we call him Wilbur Junior Junior—can already count to one hundred."

"Oh wow, that's great, Wilbur. He's in what, fourth grade now?"

"Yeah, they kept him back last year; I think because he's small for his age."

Gracie's not even two yet and can recite her ABCs, count to twenty, and speaks in sentences.

I think she's intellectually exceptional because that runs in my family. Plus, I read to her a lot, usually while we're watching *Hee Haw* or *Dukes of Hazzard* reruns on TV. All that stimulation really seems to help with the development of language skills.

Last Sunday, our daughter, Maggie, brought Gracie over to visit us and Gracie said, just as plain as day: "Grampa, please read about guns and guitars again."

I'm so excited. Soon she'll be reading *Uncle Hank's Trading Post* to me.

I think Gracie is going to be an exceptional athlete someday. She was walking at nine months and running at ten months.

Last weekend, I took her over to the Smalltown IGA for a "big girl treat" to reward her for giving up her pacifier.

She made it from the store entrance, past the fruits and vegetables, beyond the dairy products, all the way to the Slim Jims in 4.2 seconds. I think that might be a record.

Did I mention that my granddaughter is cuter than two speckled puppies? That, I had nothing to do with. She gets that from her Grammy.

My buddies, Roy, Munzie and Barney have very cute granddaughters, too, but Gracie is the most beautiful little girl I've seen since her mother was born. I know you're thinking I'm seeing her through the biased eyes of a doting grandfather, but Gracie really is the cutest ever. You don't have to take my word for it. The next time I see you, I'll treat you to a three-hour slide show of the Gracie photos on my smart phone.

You'd think such a perfect little girl would be "spoiled" by her grandfather, as if he were wrapped around her little finger, but that's not the case. Grampa has rules.

She knows she has to promise to eat her dinner right *after* the hot fudge sundae with whipped cream and nuts—just like Grampa.

ROB ENGELMAN LIKES TO TALK

Every year, my buddies, Roy and Ted, and I rent a hunting cabin over in Plymouth, Maine from a really nice couple, Rob and Yvette Engelman.

The Maine rifle season for deer starts two weeks earlier than the season here in Smalltown, so we like to go over there and get practiced up on the beer drinking, poker playing, storytelling . . . oh, and hunting. An extra estrogen-free week doesn't hurt our feelings either.

Rob and Yvette are dyed-in-the-wool Republicans—you know, smart folks who believe that able-bodied Americans should work hard and not expect the government to take care of their every need.

Rob is a talker—I mean a real "Chatty Cathy," and tells good stories. He could sell ice cubes to an Eskimo, which is evidenced by the fact that Yvette is an attractive woman, way out of Rob's league. He did some fast-talking to land her.

Rob and Yvette live in a nice home close to the cabin we rent, so Rob comes over to visit from time to time, usually to deliver something like candles during a power outage or a roll or two of toilet paper that Yvette thought we might need. I wonder sometimes if it is her way of garnering a little quiet time for herself.

We love Rob's stories, though I suspect he embellishes at times. The buck he shot in 1984 has gained 30 pounds since we first heard about it in 2011.

Yvette is a good sport, so I decided to take advantage of that and an old- time Maine story to have some fun at Rob's expense.

This past deer season, Rob came over to our cabin and was telling a story which insinuated that he was quite the ladies' man in his younger days. The door was open.

"Well, Rob," I said, "Ted here may not look like much, but he has a way with women. In fact, he was just telling us that over the past few deer seasons, he's had his way with every woman on this camp road except one."

"You don't say; every woman on this road," Rob replied.

"All but one," I repeated.

Rob excused himself shortly thereafter and headed back to his house.

"Yvette," he said. "You won't believe what Joe just told me."

"Oh really?" Yvette played along.

"Yes. He said that Ted had made love to every woman on our camp road except one. What do you make of that?"

Yvette looked thoughtful. "Well, he is a charming devil," she replied. "I'll bet it's that stuck up Marion Pendelton in the red house by the lake."

MY BIG BROTHER IS A SLEEPWALKER

I know many of you find most of my stories hard to believe, and for good reason. I make a lot of this stuff up.

This story, however, is based on the truth (though there may be a few embellishments caused by gaps in my memory bank and in the interest of a good story).

My older brother, Sam, and I grew up in a big family and a small apartment. We shared not only a bedroom, but a bed. That worked out just fine until we were teenagers.

It is sometimes entertaining to live with a person who is not always awake when he seems to be. Sam would often walk, talk, and perform other bodily functions while engaged in wide-eyed sleep.

When Sam was about sixteen, he woke one night at about midnight and needed to make water. To get to the only bathroom in our home, you had to pass through the living room and into the bath. On this night, Sam made it through the room our sisters shared and into the room where Mom was watching Johnny Carson. It did not go over well when my brother lifted the seat cushion of Dad's overstuffed chair as though it was a toilet seat and proceeded to relieve himself. Mom shrieked like a cat in a street fight and my brother was soon awake, embarrassed, and wet.

At seventeen, I was a high school senior and worked as a meat cutter at Dad's Smalltown IGA store.

One evening, Sam was sleeping in our bed while I was sitting at the small desk in the bedroom writing a fascinating paper on the life cycle of a roundworm.

Suddenly, Sam started speaking to me. "Hey Joe, Mrs. Leonard said your hamburger smelled like a skunk, but I told her maybe so, but so did her breath."

I decided to have some fun with the situation.

"Thanks Sam," I said. "That's weird, because she told me you smelled like a manure-covered goat."

"She said what? You wait until I see her again."

"See who?" I was testing him.

"See Mrs. . . . , uhmm, I don't know. What were you talking about?"

My brother was awake and, when I told him of our conversation, we shared a good laugh.

In 1967, Sam enrolled as a student at a nearby Community College right here in town. I finally had the bedroom to myself . . . for one semester.

It turns out that money was tight and my brother had to give up the apartment he shared with his buddy, Steve Hutchinson, and, along with it, his bachelor pad lifestyle. This led to problems.

There were a couple of times Sam, in a semi-conscious state, mistook me for one of his college girl sleep-overs. I nearly lost my virtue and my brother went to bed with me and woke up with a black eye.

ELLA IS ONE COOL BABY

My youngest granddaughter, Ella, is as cool as a Canadian winter. She's my fourth grandkid. You've met Hanson, Sumner, and Gracie, so you know they are all special. Each of them is smarter, more charming and better looking than the amazing grandchildren of my buddies, Barney, Munzie, Walt, Ted and Roy. Not bragging, just being honest.

Ella is three months old and eats, sleeps, smiles and, in general, lives life to its fullest. She possesses the beauty and grace of a princess and, consequently, has the appropriate court of servants and handmaidens at her beck and call.

Ella is exceptionally bright—being partially of Wright heritage—but, of course, doesn't speak English yet. I often wonder what she thinks of the people in her little world.

Sometimes, she must think: *I heard you the first time. Remember? I'm younger than you. My hearing is excellent. Why do you keep repeating the obvious?*

"She's such a pretty girl. Yes she is. She's such a pretty girl. Yes she is. She's such a pretty girl. Yes she is."

And what's up with that high-pitched voice? Dad, it's embarrassing. You sound like a girl—an annoyingly shrill, little girl. The dog hides under the couch because it hurts his ears. Frankly, I'd join him there if I could. And by the way, if you keep pounding on my back right after I eat, I swear I'll spit up all over your favorite "Hillary 2016" shirt . . . again.

Mom, it's becoming very apparent that you don't understand me . . . already. You were an infant once. Don't you remember anything about what it was like?

"Oh, my pretty baby is smiling at her Mommy. Yes she is. Yes she is. Yes she is."

Oh great; here we go again. I'm not smiling. I have gas. My belly hurts. I need to toot. (Phhhhhhhht) Oh, that feels better.

"Oh, that's stinky. Did my baby girl make a poop in her diaper? Did you do that? Did you baby girl? Did you baby girl?"

No, Mom, I tooted. You'll know it when I poop. You've been changing my dirty diaper four times a day for three months now. I can't believe you don't know the difference.

"Who's Grammy's best baby girl? Who's Grammy's best baby girl? Who's Grammy's best baby girl?"

That would be me, Grammy. I'm your only baby girl. Oh, and I know you're trying to entertain me, but could you stop sticking out your tongue and making that motorboat sound? You're spitting on me. And do you really have to kiss me every ten seconds? I know I'm adorable, but enough is enough.

Most of the people around me act a little crazy. I'd run away (if I could walk). There is that one guy, though, who's pretty amazing. He's a bit like a bigger version of me. He's bald, soft, and chubby and, like me, appreciates a good mid-day nap. He's like an island of sanity in a sea of madness. That Grampa dude is awesome.

IT SEEMED LIKE A COMPLIMENT TO ME

As I may have mentioned before, some of my family and friends accuse me of being a bit of a smart aleck. I remember one time, one of them said: "Shut up or you'll get a whoopin' you won't forget anytime soon, you #%&@S big wise (aleck)."

"Okay Mom," I replied.

Folks claim that I say things that are embarrassing or even hurtful. I swear I'm not mean, I'm just misunderstood.

Take for example, last October. I was at the checkout counter at the IGA when my daughter's old high school friend, Amy, steps into the line behind me. I was happy to see her. She had spent a lot of time at our home as a youngster and I hadn't seen her in years.

"Hi Amy, good to see you," I said.

"Great to see you too, Mr. Wright. How are you? You look great," she lied. She was all smiles and giggles. I could tell she was genuinely happy to see me.

"I'm fine, Amy. Thanks. You look good, too."

The conversation was going well. And then it fell apart.

"Look at us," I said, rubbing my protruding abdomen. "We kinda look alike, but I gotta tell you, Amy, you look a lot better with a baby bump than I do."

Now that's a cute little compliment, right?

Amy blushed. "Uhm, Mr. Wright, I'm not pregnant."

Her smile disappeared.

I blushed. It was awkward.

My buddy Munzie is prone to doing embarrassing stuff himself.

He stopped by the house last summer, all spun up because our mutual friend, Roy's wife, Mimi, had gotten on his case when he walked into the bathroom at her house without knocking and caught her on the throne. She was mortified and read him the riot act about good manners, courtesy, brains, and several other traits she accused him of lacking. Munzie felt bad and left her home almost immediately.

A week later, he's at my door expressing his regret and feeling like she would never forgive him. I reassured him.

"Munzie, I'm pretty sure she's over it. After you left, I told her I was certain it was an accident and you didn't mean to walk in on her. She said she knew you did it on purpose; there was no way you didn't know what you were doing. 'He's not as dumb as he looks,' she said. But I stuck up for you, Munzie. I said you absolutely were."

I try to be a good friend.

And I try to be a sensitive guy, too.

Like there was this time I stopped by the office to get my truck route for the day only to find Tammy, the young dispatcher, in tears.

"What's wrong, Tammy?" I inquired.

"Justin dumped me. He said he don't love me no more," she said, water spewing from her eyes and nostrils.

I sat down beside her and put my arm around her in a fatherly way. I was searching for the perfect words of consolation when, as if heaven sent, they came to me.

"Tammy, I know this seems like the end of the world to you right now, but you'll get over Justin. And some day, you'll find a guy who deserves and appreciates you for the sweet girl you are . . . a guy who isn't shallow and understands that looks aren't everything."

Now tell me that's not a Hallmark moment.

And then there was the time I was having breakfast with my brother, K.C., over at the Miss Smalltown Diner. I told Eva, our waitress, not to bring any toast or potatoes with my bacon and eggs because I was watching my carbs.

"Oh, I get it, Joe. With all this food around, I've put on 15 pounds since I started working here eight months ago," Eva replied.

"Oh, don't worry about getting a little chunky. You look good with a little extra junk in the trunk."

She slapped me in the back of my head, knocking my "Sexy Grandpa" hat into K.C.'s coffee.

It seemed like a compliment to me.

I COLLECT COOL STUFF

I've always liked to collect things. I'm a collector; the little woman says I'm a hoarder. Maybe, but I've got some cool stuff.

My favorite stuff once belonged to the most important men in my life. My mother's dad, my Pepére, had a favorite finish hammer that I watched him use to build furniture and cabinets in the house where I grew up. I have that hammer now and feel his presence every time I use it. For some reason, though, that magic hammer, in my hand, rarely drives a finish nail without bending it in half.

My Grampa Wright carried a Colt .45 pistol as an Army officer during three wars. He wore the Army Expert Pistol Badge as evidence of his skill with his sidearm. Dad gave me Gramp's pistol a few years ago and, at twenty yards, I rarely hit the target, though I once knocked it down by hitting the small post (six inches below the bottom of the target) that it was attached to.

Dad shot a lot of big deer in his heyday. He was a heck of a hunter. Most of his many trophy bucks, including several weighing well over two hundred pounds, were killed with his .300 Savage. I carry that rifle now and I can often nail the bullseye in a paper target with it. I just don't seem to see deer when I'm hunting with Dad's rifle. I'm thinking maybe Dad ventured out a little farther from the camp than I do.

At home, I'm under a lot of pressure to clean some of my collectables out of the attic. I just don't have anything I want to part with.

I've got boxes of magazines Winnie thinks I don't need. Many of these journals date back to my childhood and I can't help but wonder if I'll need them someday. What if I need to do research on Alfred E. Neuman or Hugh Hefner?

Before Bic lighters, nearly every business passed out matchbooks as part of their marketing campaign because nearly every adult American smoked—in the house, the car, restaurants, the doctor's office and church. I have hundreds of matchbooks and, from time to time, I enjoy looking at them because they bring back memories—Dr. Parker puffing on a Camel while checking my eyes, the glow of Father Trafton's Lucky Strike from inside the confessional, or my Nana with an Old Gold Filter hanging from her mouth as she fed my little sister a bottle.

I've got boxes of old bottle caps in the attic. These are not the screw type you see on today's beverage containers. These are the old crimp on, metal caps that required a bottle opener. I saved the Nehi Root Beer cap from the treat Uncle Jack bought me after I hit my first—and only—Little League home run. Peeno Lester was a giant at twelve years old and could seemingly throw a baseball 90 MPH. He also had a scary curve ball. We were losing by one run. I was up with two on base and two outs. I remember my only goal was to survive. When Peeno's curve approached my head, I ducked to get out of the way and my bat accidentally swung as I was falling and I hit the ball over third base and drove in the winning runs. I was a hero, but more importantly, I didn't suffer brain damage.

I have a Moxie bottle cap to remind me of the time I chugged a sixteen-ounce Moxie at the Bag Balm Prom to show Kimmy Peters how cool and tough I was. I puked on her pink dress.

I have a Coca-Cola cap that reminds me of the day I made the wooden rack that displays my bottle caps to this day.

My favorite collectable is the Ballantine Ale bottle cap —even though it has a little red stain on it—from the night Winnie and I made our son, Jake. It chokes me up to think about it. We were at the New Moon Drive-in Theater, watching (or, at least, listening to)

Smokey and the Bandit when I got excited during one of the chase scenes and spilled ketchup all over the backseat of my Chevy Vega.

THESE ARE A FEW OF MY FAVORITE THINGS

Raindrops on roses? Whiskers on kittens? Sure, those things are cute, I guess but they don't make my list of favorite things. Not even close.

I like a good joke. Don't send it to me all typed out in an email. I want to see how you tell it. It's all in the presentation. The lamest joke, told well—live and in person—is far more entertaining than the most hilarious written quip. My younger brother, K.C., is a good storyteller. It is fun to hear him tell a joke because no one enjoys his punch lines more than he. One would think he was hearing his own story for the first time as he usually laughs harder—a high-pitched hiccup of a laugh—than anyone in the room.

My buddy, Munzie, is also an entertaining joke teller; not because he's good at it, but because usually murders the story or the punch line.

Munzie and I play together in a bluegrass band. Once we were on a stage which had a deer head mounted on the side wall. We finished a song and my friend stepped up to the microphone to add some humor to the show. "So, Joe," he said. "What do you call a no eye deer?"

I was stumped at first because I knew the riddle, but recognized something was wrong with the question. After a moment, I figured it out and replied. "You mean 'what do you call a deer with no eyes?'" I asked, laughing as I spoke.

"Oh yeah Joe, what do you call a deer with no eyes?"

"No eye deer," I replied.

The crowd roared, not at Munzie's joke, but at his botched delivery.

My favorite food is a good burger. Not one of those turkey or tofu burgers the little woman tries to sneak into me from time to time; I like a juicy twenty-percent fat, beef burger smothered with melted cheddar, bacon, fried onions, and mayonnaise. And don't forget the fries. I know I shouldn't eat that stuff, but I'll die young, fat, and happy. There's something to be said for that.

I like beer, too. I'm not a big fan of those fruity microbrews. I like Lite beer. That's diet beer, so I can drink lots of them. My friend Barney says: "If you weren't supposed to drink thirty a day, they wouldn't make 30-packs." Try drinking thirty North Trail Blueberry Maple Honey Clover Ales in a day. There's good reason they don't package those in anything larger than a six-pack.

My favorite place is "upta camp." It's the ideal place to hang out with the guys. I'm allowed to swear, lie, burp, toot, stink, and eat seven-day-old leftover venison stew. (I am careful to scrape the mold off the top before I heat it up.)

I like Pepsi—Diet Pepsi, of course, because I'm very weight conscious. Even Diet Pepsi is a little too sweet though, so I often cut the saccharinity by diluting the soda pop—ideally with Black Velvet. My pal, Roy, and I have dubbed our favorite cocktail "Pepsi Gold." Pepsi Gold is tasty at any time of day which is a good thing since Roy's favorite mantra is "You can't drink all day if you don't start in the morning."

One of my favorite pastimes is deer hunting. Winnie doesn't understand that. "You couldn't pay me a million dollars to go deer hunting," she'll cackle. I'm okay with her staying home.

Hours of sitting a tree stand, swaying with the howling breeze, the wind chill at a balmy 10° below zero, watching with excitement as Mother Nature does her magic (how else would I know that the average oak drops three acorns per hour on a chilly November morning), waiting half a day for a big buck that never shows . . . now that's living!

My favorite human beings happen to be related—or married—to me. I guess I'm just lucky that those people are all smart, charming, kind, thoughtful, and beautiful. Above all, I enjoy the company of my grandkids, Hanson, Sumner, Gracie, and Ella. They love me unconditionally. They don't care that I'm fat, wrinkled, stinky, and sometimes a bit crotchety. All they know is that I love them, pay attention to them, give them tractor rides, act foolish for them, and buy them toys. For me, a hug from Hanson, Sumner, Gracie or Ella trumps raindrops on roses every time.

IF I WERE THE VOICE ON YOUR GPS

Generally, I avoid all the newfangled electronic gadgets that the young kids use. They confuse me and complicate my life. I still have a "flip phone" and it's not a "smart phone." I refuse to carry around a gizmo that's smarter than I am. I guess that makes mine a "dumb phone." My phone is for . . . wait for it . . . making phone calls.

I did break down, though, and buy one of those Global Positioning System navigational devices for my pickup truck and I must admit it is some handy. There's this lady in there with a soft, sexy voice who lets me know when and where to turn. I call her "Gigi." Trust me, there are plenty of people in my life—Winnie, my boss, my buddies Barney and Roy—who are happy to tell me where to go, but only Gigi sounds like she is flirting with me in the process.

I need the GPS. You see, Winnie is smarter than I am in almost every way, but asking her to read a road map is like asking a Holstein to solve a calculus equation.

"Okay, go about an inch, and when you get to the little red dot, go to the right. Oh, no, no, I mean go to the left. That's this way, right?" (She points to the right.) "Then go about two and a half inches and, when you get to the big red dot, go straight over the blue thing, I think it might be a river, and then go to the right . . . I think."

Gigi, on the other hand, would sound like this: "In 400 feet, turn right onto Bent Culvert Road." And then in exactly 400 feet she would seductively say: "Turn right onto Bent Culvert Road."

After I successfully completed the right-hand turn, Gigi would give me a heads up. "Continue straight on Bent Culvert Road for approximately one-half mile, then cross the Teddy Kennedy Bridge and continue onto Route 100, the Ronald Reagan Memorial Highway."

If I missed that right hand turn, Gigi would patiently guide me through three consecutive left hand turns to get me back to the point where I could turn right onto Bent Culvert Road.

I'd like to be the voice in someone's GPS, but I'm afraid I wouldn't be as kind or patient as Gigi.

Imagine a gravely voice with a bad attitude guiding you to the Ronald Reagan Memorial Highway.

"In 400 feet, take a right onto Bent Culvert Road."

A few seconds later: "Hang a right on Bent Culvert."

"You missed it, idiot. I told you twice to take a Christly right. Alright, now you gotta do a U-turn when you can . . . you know, like on the *Dukes of Hazzard*."

Once you made the illegal turn, I'd instruct you again. "Alright, Bozo, pay attention this time. In 200 feet, hang a left onto Bent Culvert Road. Okay . . . now!"

Assuming you negotiated the turn successfully, I'd congratulate you.

"Alright, you got it right this time. I guess you're not a *total* idiot."

I'd then resume my helpful guidance. "Just keep headin' straight. Think you can handle that? In about half a mile, keep goin' straight over the Teddy Kennedy Bridge. You're *not* a Kennedy, so don't drift too far to the *left* or you'll end up in the drink."

Minutes later.

"Alright, you've left the Kennedy Bridge and have reached the Ronald Reagan Highway. You are finally on the right path. Everything will be alright now."

I DON'T LIVE AS DANGEROUSLY AS I ONCE DID

Guys do a lot of stupid stuff. We are responsible for most of the bad things in this world—war, crime, NASCAR, and the World Wrestling Federation. It's not our fault, it's the testosterone.

When I was a little bugger, I'd get up a full head of steam on my Big Wheel and crash it into the Lincoln Log cabin my big brother, Sam, had just spent three hours building. (Before Legos, many toys were made of wood.) Why would I do such a thing? Because I was boy—a miniature guy—and already had testosterone in my veins which means I would do stupid stuff, which seemed like fun at the time, without thinking about the consequences.

I, of course, not only scraped my knee when my Big Wheel rolled over on the asphalt driveway, and nearly had my left eye taken out by a flying Lincoln Log, but I got my backside kicked by my older brother. You'd think I'd have learned a lesson. Of course, I didn't. I'm a guy and testosterone makes me stupid.

Smalltown is a ski town. It snows eight months a year so we ski. On a hill, a short walk from my childhood home, is a really big ski jump from which sixteen year old guys with way more male hormones than brains fly with a wooden slat (in those days), attached to each foot. It's fun . . . if you don't die. I was never a ski jumper, but one February morning, Munzie, Barney, Roy and I decided to see how far a ten-foot toboggan laden with four thirteen-year-olds could fly off a forty meter jump. It turns out the flight was great fun. The landing . . . not so much. We were shocked to discover how little control we had over our hardwood vehicle once it landed on a downhill patch of glare ice. It was very hard on our backsides because our ash was not padded. There were lots of trees lining the edges of the landing hill and our toboggan found the biggest one. Our driver, Munzie, never found his front teeth.

My twenties were really dangerous. My hormones were raging; I was old enough to drive a 400-horsepower death machine, and I consumed massive quantities of cheap beer. To make things worse, it turns out that twenty-something girls are not much smarter than the boys after drinking large amounts of Pabst Blue Ribbon or Sloe Gin and, while less likely to drive 120 miles per hour down a twisted mountain road, were impressed by idiots, like me, who did.

Thinking back, I'm not sure how my buddies and I survived to reach thirty. I guess God selects several testosterone-infused morons to survive in order for our species to continue. He or she apparently does so without regard to the effect on gene pool quality.

Now that I'm closer to sixty than thirty, I've noticed I'm more careful than in my younger years. I guess that something to do with that "Low T" condition I hear about on TV commercials. The ads warn of the devastating symptoms of "Low T."

"If you would rather eat Whoopie Pies than make whoopee, if you'd rather take a nap in your La-Z-Boy than a victory lap in the number 42 Chevy, if you tune to ESPN and would rather watch Dan Patrick than Danica Patrick, if you are afraid of your little woman, because she can now kick your butt, you may suffer from a serious medical condition known as Low T."

I'm sure I am affected by Low T, but honestly, I'm really not suffering at all.

Please pass me another Whoopie Pie.

MY COLONOSCOPY

Dr. Braley told me it was time for my first colonoscopy when I turned fifty and he told me again when I turned fifty-one and again when I turned fifty-two and fifty-three and fifty-four. At 55, I told him I was pretty sure I didn't need one because it sounded like a pain in the rear.

"But Joe," he explained, "Colon cancer kills. If we find it early, we can kill it before it kills you. You can't put it off any longer."

I thought about Winnie, the kids, the grandkids, beer, Black Velvet, Slim Jims, Jack Link's Teriyaki Beef Jerky, and how much I'd miss them all—so I finally agreed.

Doc Braley wrote me a prescription for something with a fancy medical name like crapowtinablast *emulsion*. Now that I've used it, I call it "Orange Flush Nuclear Explosion." He told me to eat nothing but a few hard candies for twenty-four hours prior to my procedure.

I said: "What? You mean nothing between meals except Wintogreen Lifesavers?"

"No, Joe, nothing at all but a few hard candies. And starting at about noon on the day before your colonoscopy, drink a gallon of this orange emulsion."

He handed me the prescription.

"Can I mix it with Smirnoff's?"

"No, and stay close to the toilet. This stuff works fast."

I ate Lifesavers, pretending they were morsels of rib eye and baked potato. It didn't work. I was starving.

I called Dr. Braley. "You were pulling my leg, weren't you? You jokester. You had me going there for a while. 'Nothing but Lifesavers for a day.' You got me good that time, Doc."

"No Joe, I wasn't kidding. And don't forget the *crapowtinablast*."

So, at noon, I drank my gallon of "Orange Flush Explosion" and waited. Five minutes lapsed and nothing.

"I knew it. This stuff doesn't work on guys who eat jalapeño peppers and deer liver for breakfast. At minute number six, I felt a strange gurgling sensation in my gut. I did the forty-yard dash in 3.8 seconds and I'd have made it all the way to the toilet in time if the cat hadn't decided to do Pilates stretches in my path.

There was significant thrust factor in that initial movement. Had I not held onto the toilet seat for all I was worth, I'm sure I'd have been launched like an astronaut to the ceiling. Anyway, eight hours and forty-seven trips to the commode later, my bowels were clean as a whistle . . . and, by the way, with enough fluid pressure, one can whistle from that end, too.

So, early the next morning, I was off to see Dr. Hineepeeker, who verbally walked me through the colonoscopy.

"So, Mr. Wright, we'll give you something to relax you and you won't feel a thing."

She showed me a tube that looked like a five-foot garter snake and told me what she'd be doing with it.

"I don't think so," I replied. "I don't even like Dr. Braley's gigantic finger up there."

"It'll be fine. And best of all, if we see any little polyps, we have little blades right in this tube that'll snip them right off."

"Dr. Hineepeeker, you don't seem to be listening. I don't even like Dr. Braley's giant, unmanicured finger up there."

"Just roll on your side Mr. Wright and we'll get started. You can watch on the TV monitor if you'd like."

"No thank you. Are you kidding me? No way. And by the way, before you ask, I don't want to watch your cousin's hemorrhoidectomy either."

I think Dr. Hineepeeker liked me. Shortly after my humorous comment, I heard her order the anesthesia guy to "give him a little bonus."

The next thing I remember, I was in the recovery room.

The nurse's assistant was offering me muffins and coffee when Dr. H entered and complimented me. "You did a great job with the prep work, Mr. Wright. You are the only patient we ever had use the *crapowtinablas*t and lose half his body weight."

NO VANITY PLATES FOR ME

Lots of folks have special license plates on their car or truck and while I'm intrigued by trying to figure some of them out, I've never been inclined to purchase vanity plates for my pickup. Mostly because I'm too cheap to pay the extra thirty bucks.

I guess people put vanity plates on their rigs for a variety of reasons. Some want to draw attention to themselves or some accomplishment. About a month ago, my buddy, Roy, and I were chewing the fat—literally—down at the Miss Smalltown Diner when we saw a shiny new Corvette pull into the parking lot. The Massachusetts license tag read QTRBAK. As the driver pried his oversized gut out from behind the steering wheel, it was apparent that if he was ever a quarterback, it was thirty years and about 40,000 beers ago.

I suppose some drivers just want to tell us something about themselves. They—like our "friends" on Facebook who tell us when they eat a bowl of chili and pass gas—think we care. Last Tuesday I was following a late model Ford Explorer with a plate that read IDOC. I guess this optometrist wanted me to know his profession in case I lost a contact lens while driving at seventy miles per hour.

Some vanity plates are quite clever. My favorite of all time was on the bumper of a 1968 VW bus which was painted sunshine yellow and decorated with flowers, rainbows, peace signs and stickers which encouraged others to "Give Peace a Chance" and "Make Love, Not War." The registration tag had me baffled (it nearly drove me over the edge). It read PV34 PV3P. I practically had to stand on my head to figure out that the owners were, not surprisingly, fans of the Grateful Dead.

Ava Fairbanks, the wealthiest woman in St. Jamesboro, thinks she's the local equivalent of Julia Roberts. Her Mercedes sports a plate that reads PRETY WMN.

Almost every parent is proud of their children, but I think we've all been annoyed by that SOCCR MOM whose Volvo wagon is plastered with bumper stickers that let us know "My Daughter is an Honor Student."

Jake Mitchell's camo pickup truck has a GUT DEER plate, an NRA sticker, and another which reads "My Dropout is Dating Your Honor Student" (cleaned up for public consumption).

Sports fans often pay for vanity tags. John Dickenson drives a Subaru Outback covered with stickers. There's one that claims: "Yankees Suck," another that reads: "Boston Red Sox–2004, 2007 and 2013 World Champions," a "dangling socks" sticker, and one with the familiar Red Sox "B". His license plate is SOX FAN. Really John? Good thing you paid an extra thirty bucks for that tag.

I think the little woman has, at times, been tempted to get me a special plate. Once in a while, we visit our son, Jake, in the city and we stay at a hotel. They always want to know my vehicle registration number at check-in and, I must admit, if Winnie were to order me a fancy plate, it would be easier to remember DIMWIT than 45376LT.

A GUY'S LIFE IS SIMPLE

Not all men of my gender are guys. Most are—especially Smalltown men.

From what I've seen of the folks that visit Smalltown from away, city men are more likely to have collared shirts that are made of something other than flannel; they have several pair of shoes; they don't seem to own work boots; they have fancy hair that was cut by someone other than themselves and with a tool other than sheep shears; and consequently, they never wear a John Deere ballcap. Those are not guys.

Guys like me have a limited wardrobe. The clothes I wear include two pair of Wrangler bluejeans, three T-shirts, two flannel shirts, five pair of socks, four pair of skivvies (tighty whities, by the way), a pair of work boots, and one pair of Converse All-Stars I bought in high school.

It's good that I have plenty of clothes because I have no idea how to operate the washer and dryer. It seems I shrunk a Cashmere sweater thirty years ago (it was an accident . . . really), and I haven't been allowed to do laundry since. You can't imagine how distraught I am over this.

Anyway, my point is, when the little woman had to go stay with her sister for three weeks to take care of her, following a complicated hemorrhoidectomy, I had plenty to wear during those twenty-one days without doing laundry. The math is quite simple—three days with BVDs right side out, two days inside out. That's twenty days, leaving just one commando day in three weeks.

Winnie seems to worry a lot more than I do. She frets over things I can't imagine losing sleep over like:

Moving the furniture—Winnie seems to quickly get bored with the scenery in our living room. Every six weeks, or so, I need a map to find my La-Z-Boy. I don't get it. As long as I can lean back, there's room for the footrest to pop up, and I can reach the TV tray that holds my beer, I'm happy.

The Kids—When the kids were growing up, I was occasionally left in charge of them. That ended when I lost track of Maggie at the Kingdom County Fair. She, for reasons I'll never understand, got bored with the giant pumpkin weigh-ins and wandered off. The little woman was some upset with me even though that nice carnie guy not only took good care of our little princess, but paid her three bucks for helping him tack new balloons up on his dart board. That's pretty good money for a six year old.

Food Safety—Winnie throws away a lot of perfectly good food. She has this three-day rule. If it has been in the fridge for more than three days (two if it contains mayonnaise), into the trash it goes. She won't even feed it to the Beagle who eats four-day old road kill and his own frozen poop. I try to explain to her that at hunting camp, we scrape the mold off the two-week-old venison stew, heat it up, and enjoy. She just rolls her eyes and reminds me again that I'm a moron.

Offending Friends—Women are thin-skinned. Winnie will cry for days because her friend, Henrietta, said she looks better since she put on a few pounds. I don't even whimper when my brother, K.C., tells me I look like a warthog and smell even worse. I know he means it in the kindest way.

I'm glad I wasn't born with lady parts and, as a man, I'm glad I'm a guy.

I HATE LOUSY SERVICE

I'm nothing special; but if you work in a job that provides a service I can get somewhere else, you'd damn well better treat me like I'm Tom Brady or Homer Simpson.

Last Monday, my buddy, Munzie, and I went over to the Miss Smalltown Diner for the liver and onions special. Eunice Darling was waiting tables and was, apparently, having a bad afternoon. She greeted us at our duct tape patched booth with: "Whatcha want, and make it quick. I'm busier than a crow on trash pick-up day."

"I want to see a menu, Eunice," I replied. "And a smile would be nice."

"Oh for goodness sake Joe, you don't need a blasted menu. You can barely read anyway and you know you're gettin' the special, you cheap old bugger."

"Well, maybe Munzie wants to see a menu, Eunice."

"Oh sure Joe, like Munzie's smart enough to make a decision. He's just gonna order whatever you have, so just order the liver and onions and let me move on to the next table of idiots."

I grabbed my jacket and slid across the vinyl bench, which, by the way, makes noises like I'm passing gas when my dungarees are damp from the rain. "We're outta here Munzie. If I wanna be treated like a cow flop, I would rather go see that waitress down to the Railway Café and give *her* my tip."

"Oh no, Joe," Eunice yelled as we headed for the door. "What will I do without that extra fifty cents?"

Eunice doesn't seem to understand that if you want that fifty cent tip, you've got to treat customers like they're special.

It's no wonder the U.S. Postal Service is on the verge of financial collapse.

I was in the Smalltown Post Office a week before Halloween because I needed to mail a small package of candy corn to our granddaughter, Gracie. There was a line of a dozen, or so, folks waiting for service from the one government worker behind the counter.

After a forty-five minute wait—mind you, this is at two on a Tuesday afternoon, not exactly rush hour—I get to the counter.

"I'd like to mail this package," I explained.

"Priority, parcel post, or media mail?" Ralph barked at me.

"I don't know."

"Is it a book?" Ralph rolled his eyes.

"No."

"Where is it going?"

"Boston," I replied. "Just like it says on the address label."

"If you want it to get there overnight it will be $22.46. You can send it Priority Mail for $7.20."

"$22.46? It's a one-dollar bag of candy for my granddaughter."

"Well, isn't she the lucky little girl?" Ralph said, with tongue in cheek.

That was it. I'd taken all the lousy service I was going to accept from Ralph.

"Look Ralph, I'm paying for a service here and I expect to be treated with kindness and courtesy. I don't have to use the U.S. Postal Service to mail this package. I've got other choices. I chose you only because I'm a patriot and a taxpayer, which means my tax dollars pay your salary and benefits."

I could feel my face turning red and the veins in my neck bulging. "So, if you don't like your job, get out of here, and we'll hire one of the millions of people smarter than you who would be happy to take your place and would treat me like they appreciate my business."

The lobby, apparently full of fellow taxpayers, erupted in cheers and applause.

Ralph, without changing his attitude a bit, slapped a stamp on my package and said, "Parcel Post. It will be there in 7 to 10 days. That's $4.95. Next."

I learned something on that cold, rainy October day. I learned to plan ahead when I want to mail goodies to my grandkids. I also learned that with enough duct tape and enough fellow disgruntled "employers," a postal worker holding a sign that reads: "Customer Training in Progress" can be strapped to the flagpole outside the Smalltown Post Office.

SOMETIMES I LIE

I try to be honest. As a kid, my momma would wash my mouth with Lifebuoy if she caught me telling a lie. I hated that.

But, sometimes, it's just easier to fib than to tell the truth.

Almost every time I run into an old classmate down at the IGA, they say something like: "Hey Joe, good to see you. How are you?"

I'm almost certain they don't really care how I am and are asking to be polite, or even more likely, out of habit; so I almost always answer with one word: "Fine."

Then I pretend to give a damn and ask them how they are doing.

It is easier and kinder to say "I'm fine" than to go on about that "annoying itch" caused by what my old man calls "piles."

And folks probably don't want to hear about the belly cramps I get after a big feed of baked beans and deer liver.

And trust me; you're better off if I spare you the details of my "productive cough." I'm sure you don't want me to describe what my cough produces.

Sometimes I start the day with a lie. "Good morning," I'll reply to a similar greeting.

Often, it's not a good morning at all, but what am I to say?

If I was to be honest, some days would start with a less-than-pleasant reply. "Well good for you. I'm so happy you're having a good morning. As for me, my day started with my right foot in a puddle of warm, regurgitated Kibbles and Bits deposited next to my bed by the cat. After cleaning up that mess, I discovered, the hard way, that the milk I poured into my coffee was three weeks old and I had to clean my own puke off the carpet. After all the vomiting and cleaning, I was running late for work and discovered my truck battery was dead. I had to wait to be jump-started because Winnie was at Zumba class. She finally gets home at about ten o'clock after having an after-exercise double mocha latté and a jelly donut with her friend, Mimi, and I get to work four hours late where I'm greeted by my irate boss. So, no, it's not a good morning."

It's easier and nicer to just lie and say: "Good morning."

I've found there are other times when dishonesty is the best policy. Last Tuesday, the little woman asked me to name the best day of my life, so far.

That was a tough one. I wasn't sure whether to choose our wedding day, September-something, 1977, or the day Jake was born, sometime in the spring of 1979, or the day of Maggie's arrival, December 22 of 1981 or 1982.

I certainly knew better than to say October 27, 2004 at 11:37 PM, when Kevin Foulke tossed the ball to Doug Mientkiewicz for the final out of the 2004 World Series, securing the Red Sox' first World Championship in 86 years.

I HATE MIRRORS

I don't look carefully into mirrors these days. I guess there are a couple of reasons for this behavior.

First off, I don't care all that much about my appearance. It seems like some time around my sixtieth birthday I jumped off the train to vain and decided I'm not really concerned about how I look. Besides, the little woman has kept me around for the better part of forty years now and I don't expect her to kick me to the street just because I've lost some curb appeal. She knows I'm kind of like a steamed clam. I'm not much to look at, but if you can get past that, I'm really quite enjoyable.

I do shave nearly every day, so I do look at my reflection every twenty-four hours or so, otherwise I'd lop off a chunk of my chin or nose. Still, I try not to look at myself any longer than absolutely necessary. The face in my mind's eye is far younger and more attractive than that wrinkled up mug staring back at me from the looking glass over the sink.

Since I don't pay much attention to the goober in the mirror, it would be nice if a friend, or loved one, would pay enough attention to my face to tell me when I have something hanging from it.

My buddies are not good about that. Last November, Ted and I were up to deer camp and decided to stop at a diner for the hunters' breakfast. The waitress, Tonya, was some cute.

"Mornin' darling," I said in my charming way. "I'll have a coffee."

Tonya poured my coffee, but acted funny. She was having trouble making eye contact with me. I noticed she was fine with Ted and looked at him square-on when she took his order. Ted's even homelier than I am, so I was perplexed.

"I'll have the "Hunter's Special," I said.

"How'd you like your eggs?" Tonya asked while focusing at the salt shaker two feet to my left.

"Over easy please. Do you have a problem with me, sweetheart?"

Tonya fidgeted with her pen and then pointed toward my nose without looking at me directly.

I grabbed the chrome-sided napkin dispenser and checked out my reflection. There, hanging from my right nose cave was a green booger the size of a horsefly. I removed it with a napkin and glared at my buddy.

"Jeez, Ted, why didn't you tell me I had a loogie hanging from my face?"

"I didn't want to embarrass ya, Joe," Ted explained. "It was just danglin' there and the way it was floppin' around every time ya breathed, I figured it would fall off any second."

Winnie isn't any better. One morning last July, I had eaten breakfast with her, kissed her goodbye and headed off to work.

I punched my time card and said: "Good mornin' Tiffany," to the secretary behind the desk.

"Eeew . . . gross, Joe," Tiffany shrieked. "What's that on your face? I think I just threw up in my mouth a little."

I ducked into the restroom, assuming I had another giant, green bat in the cave. I was wrong. There, plain as the nose on my face, was a wood tick, so bloated with my blood, it looked like a Concord grape hanging from my left cheek.

"Damn Winnie," I sputtered to myself. "You can find tiny ticks on Kitty through two inches of matted fur, but you don't notice a huge, purple, blood-engorged blob suspended from below my left eye?"

As painful as it might be, I guess I'll have to look at the man in the mirror a little more carefully from here on. Maybe I'll at least catch those things that are big and gross and colorful before I go out and share them with the world.

THINGS I'M NOT GOOD AT

There are a few things I'm fairly good at. I like to eat and I've become quite proficient at it. Practice makes perfect, and I'm determined to improve.

I am excellent at teaching people how to play Cribbage. I've taught a dozen or so people so well, they all beat me consistently.

The little woman says I'm a good dancer. I think her exact words were: "Joe, you cut the rug pretty well for a guy with two left feet."

There are many things, though, I'm not good at.

When Winnie and I had been married a week, or so, I shrunk her favorite sweater by two sizes. I've been banished from the laundry room ever since.

I'm also terrible at folding clothing. Winnie packs a suitcase and every article of her wardrobe looks just like it did on the Small-Mart display rack. I take lots of time and care folding my shirts and britches and packing them into my suitcase and they still look like they are straight out of the dirty clothes hamper.

Every couple of months, Winnie and I take in the all-you-can-eat buffet at the Wok the Dog Chinese restaurant in St. Jamesboro. They always offer me chopsticks and I always decline them in favor of a good, old-fashioned fork. I've seen my not-so-Asian neighbors trying to eat with sticks and they end up eating cold General Tsao's Chicken and getting rice all over themselves. I can put away four times the Pork Chow Mein as my trendy friends; I eat it while it's hot, and I don't end up looking like I have little white maggots all over my "Still Sexy at Sixty" tee shirt that I want to keep nice for my uncle's wedding coming up next summer.

There are certain things I'm picky about, and yet I'm lousy at doing those things the way I want them done.

I like a good fried egg, over-easy with a nice, runny, cholesterol-laden, yellow yolk to sop up with a butter-drenched toast. But I can never seem to cook an egg that way. I either break the yoke when I flip it, or overcook it until the yellow center resembles Play-Doh and doesn't taste much better. (Come on, admit it; you know you tasted Play-Doh as a kid.)

I've got a slightly lazy left eye, which leaves me with poor depth perception. Consequently, I can't hang a picture straight. That's a big problem for a guy who can't sit in a room containing a crooked wall hanging without getting up to straighten it.

I also have a hard time parking my camper trailer straight. I've discovered though, I'm not the only person with that problem. Every year, I'm the first to arrive at the East Bumcrack Bluegrass Festival where they tell every camper to back up perpendicular to the tree line. Mine is always the only camper parked straight. All of the others are crooked and parallel to each other. There are, apparently, a bunch of one-eyed bluegrass pickers.

I THINK I'M BECOMING MY FATHER

When I was in my twenties—a long time ago—I was sure I'd never get old. Somehow, I was going to be the first person to circumvent the aging process. I would retain the youthful appearance and physical fitness of my twenties without the use of hair dye, Rogaine, human growth hormone, Botox or surgery. I would stay young, simply because I am me and God loves me.

It ain't working out that way.

I've become a thick-around-the-middle, wrinkled, chicken-skinned, balding, gray-haired, set-in-my-ways, arthritic codger and I'm not a damned bit pleased about it.

Seems like I never feel one hundred percent healthy anymore. One week my right shoulder aches for no apparent reason and, as soon as that heals itself, the bunion on my left big toe becomes inflamed. And so on.

I get injured sometimes, too. Mind you, I'm not talking about throwing my back out by lifting a fifty-pound bag of cement mix. Sometimes reaching over to switch off the lamp next to my bed can cause me to hobble around like Amos McCoy for a week. This aging crap ain't for wimps.

And I've developed a new enemy—the mirror. Last Tuesday, I was shaving and there, looking back at me, was my father.

I don't mind having my dad's features; he's a good looking guy, like all the Wright boys. I just want to look like he did at twenty-five.

It's not just the mirror, either. I'm becoming my father in other ways too. That's not all bad, I love Ol' Dad, but I just can't believe how often I'll hear myself say something and realize I've become him.

Lately I've heard myself say things like:

"How can these kids listen to that crap? That ain't even music."

"How can you stand that hair in your eyes? You look like a damned girl."

"Kids these days don't want to work for a living. They want everything handed to 'em."

"Why don't that kid buy some pants that fit?"

"Because I said so, that's why."

"Stop crying or I'll give you something to really cry about."

Dad has a real gift for making borderline inappropriate remarks to the ladies without getting his face slapped. I haven't mastered that yet.

Once, at Luigi's Bar and Grill, Dad motioned for the young waitress, Shelli to return to our table right after she'd taken our order.

"Yes?' Shelli said.

"Oh, nothing," Ol' Dad relied. "I just wanted to see if you looked as good coming as going."

She laughed.

So how come when I told the young waitress down at Fat Anthony's: "You look good, Eva. I like a girl with a big caboose," I was rewarded with a black eye? It seemed like a compliment to me.

Maybe I'm not my father yet, after all.

AVERAGE JOE'S REVOLUTIONARY WEIGHT LOSS PLAN

I'd like to weigh less. I'd be healthier and I'm pretty sure the little woman would like a thinner husband. But I love to eat. I like beer, too.

As my girth increases, it's becoming apparent that my passion for chocolate, burgers, fries, and Pabst Blue Ribbon exceeds my longing to be thinner.

Winnie knows how I feel and tries to help. She rarely bakes cookies or pies. Unfortunately, Candi, the payroll gal at North Woods Construction where I work, loves to bake and is very good at it. I try to resist but I'm not very good at that. Winnie subscribes to a bunch of those women's magazines which are just full of ways to take off fat. She had me on the "All Spinach and Broccoli Diet" for two days until she couldn't stand the gaseous emissions any longer. I was self-propelled for several days, tooting with every step down the hallway and our home was starting to take on the odor of "Myra"—the outdoor two-seater up to camp, my Nana named it after the mean old lady in the cottage next door.

The "All Liquid Diet" didn't work out well either. I had to pee every ten minutes and gained ten pounds in a week. Winnie told me liquids only. She didn't explain that didn't include chocolate milkshakes or beer.

Then there was "The Daily Enema Program." I was allowed to eat a lot due to the daily "cleansing," but it was a pain in the . . . well, you know.

"The Grapefruit Diet" was boring and the acid nearly burned a hole through my stomach. It made me grumpy.

We tried the "No Carbs, No Fat, No Salt Diet." They should call it the "If It Tastes Good, Spit It Out Diet." You can imagine how long I stuck to that one.

Looking around, especially at Small-Mart, I've noticed there are lots of big people. I decided I'd come up with my own weight loss plan and write a book about it. I've included the book, in its entirety, in this article.

Average Joe's Revolutionary Weight Loss Plan

Chapter One: Eat Less
Do I need to explain that?

Chapter Two: Eat Better
Lay off the chocolate, chips, and cheesecake. If you really like it, you probably shouldn't eat it.

Chapter Three: Drink Less Beer
A lot less. Yes, that includes you Barney, Munzie, and Roy.

Chapter Four: Get More Exercise
Walk more—more than just from the couch to the fridge.

I'M A LOW—TECH GUY

I don't understand how all the high technology gizmos of the modern world work. Heck, I'm just beginning to comprehend how another person's voice can travel through wires and I can hear them a thousand miles away on my land line phone. I, sure as the Dickens, don't get how pictures and movies of my grandkids, Hanson, Sumner, Gracie, and Ella can travel through the air and land in my computer. That just doesn't make any sense.

I've had to learn a little about word processing, email, and even Facebook so I could share all of Average Joe's deep thoughts with all of you, but that surely doesn't mean I comprehend how it all works.

I was telling my son, Jake, that my PC has been running slowly even though my internet service through the cable company costs more than our rent did when he was born. He said my memory was getting low (like I didn't already know that). He explained that my computer didn't have enough RAM (nothing to do with sheep) to handle all the Bill Monroe and Merle Haggard songs or the hunting and fishing videos I have stored on there.

I told him there was no way I could get rid of those or the grandkid movies, so he said I could get all that stuff off my computer and store it in "the Cloud."

"Say what? Which cloud? And who's up there sorting out my stuff from everyone else's stuff?" Now I'm really confused—and worried that Jake has been spending so much time with Hanson and Sumner that he is losing his marbles.

"Don't worry Dad," he tries to reassure me. "Your stuff gets stored out there in cyberspace and you can retrieve it whenever you want to."

"But I don't want my stuff out there in space with everyone else's," I explain. "What if I want to look at a picture of my junk Chevy and I get a picture of Chevy Chase's junk? I don't want to see that."

"And I don't want Jennifer Aniston accidentally seeing pictures of me in my blaze orange hunting outfit and having lustful thoughts about me. What if it caused her to dump her boyfriend? I don't want to be a homewrecker."

Last Christmas, my kids bought me a handheld Global Positioning System gadget (because I *will not* give up my flip phone) to carry in the woods. They said they worry about me getting lost.

"I won't get lost," I said. "I've been hunting the woods from Smalltown to Island Lake for more than forty years. I know them like the back of my hand."

Well, wouldn't you know it, that November I was scaring whitetails up on Buck Mountain, and things looked different to me in part because they had cut down a lot of trees to make room for some giant windmills (don't get me started). I'll admit I got turned around because the loggers had cut down BFO, the big oak on Paul's Peak, and other landmarks I'd depended on to find my way around the woods.

I pulled the GPS from my jacket pocket and turned it on for the first time. The next thing I know, the screen showed a bright blue dot that indicated my position on Buck Mountain. *Now, how does this gizmo know where I am when I don't?* I thought to myself.

But that was no big help. I didn't need to know where I was—I was already there. I needed that rig to tell me where my truck was, so I could walk back to it and drive home to the little woman who, I was sure, was missing me something awful and pacing the floor with worry. Luckily, the sun broke through the clouds about that time and I knew its position would be to my south, because I was really hungry and it had to be around noontime, so I headed west and eventually found the old Dodge.

Jake told me I should have marked my parking spot as a waypoint on the GPS and it would have told me exactly how far and in which direction I needed to head to find my truck. *Whatever.*

TOYS HAVE CHANGED SINCE I WAS A KID

As I watch my grandchildren and their friends play with their toys, I can't help but notice how dissimilar they are to those I grew up with.

On Christmas morning, the December after I turned eight, Santa brought me an Etch A Sketch. Those of you who remember the little red rectangle know that after about three hours practice, a kid could, simply by turning the small, white knobs, draw a TV set that, if you squinted a bit, looked a little like a disfigured Etch A Sketch.

This Christmas, my nephew, Eli, received an iPad with which he can make full length movies complete with sound and special effects. With the push of a button, he can share his creation with 4,272 "friends" from Smalltown to Kyrgyzstan. He knows only 43 of these "friends" and "likes" only 13 of them. Most of these friends will never see his video because they each have thousands of "friends" they don't know posting fascinating comments about the chicken noodle or curry poodle soup they are eating.

I guess we were weird when I was growing up in the hills of Smalltown. We actually went *outdoors* to play games. We'd go into the woods, hike the hills, hide behind trees and pretend to shoot at each other with wooden toy guns.

"Bang, bang," we'd yell. "I gotcha."

"Did not."

"Did too."

"Did not; you missed me. I ducked."

"No you didn't." ("No way" hadn't yet become part of the American lexicon.) "I gotcha."

And so it would go, on and on until one of the older kids would say: "He gotcha Joey. You're dead, so just shut up."

These days the wars are conducted indoors, in front of a big screen TV with no visible guns, just hand held game controllers which allow the young warrior to fire automatic weapons, launch grenades, or rockets, and blow up entire cities with one agile thumb movement. It all looks and sounds very real and, best of all, not only trains our little ones to be *Soldiers of Fortune*, but also teaches them the violent skills required to excel at *Grand Theft Auto* and introduces them to the sadistic options for a *Thrill Kill*—all without requiring them to break a sweat or burn a calorie.

Houses were smaller and families were larger back before "the pill" and the outdoors was part of our living space. It was always easy to muster enough kids for a game of football. We ran, tackled, and blocked our way to fitness. There was no *Madden 1965* to be played in front of our black and white Sylvania TV set.

For Christmas in 1960, I got enough Lincoln Logs to build an entire village of wooden buildings and I'm guessing Santa paid about three bucks for the whole shebang. This year, Santa brought a Lego Motorhome to my grandson, Sumner. It came with motors, lights, buzzers, and more moving parts than an F-150 pickup truck. I'm guessing it set the man in the red suit back about $60. I spent four hours putting it together. (I might have assembled it in three hours had I peeked at the instructions.) Sumner played with it for three minutes after which it took him only thirty seconds to tear it apart.

MEN ARE HONEST. WOMEN LIE.

The guy who first proclaimed that "Honesty is the Best Policy" probably never lived with a woman like Winnie. If he did, he was frequently in deep doo-doo. I've lived with the little woman for more than thirty-five years now and it was only about a year ago that I figured out it is often safer to lie. I'm not sure why it took thirty-four years and dozens of fights to come to that epiphany. It may be because I'm a guy and . . . well . . . not too bright. But I am honest. Stupid and honest—a dangerous combination.

It doesn't help that I spend time with Roy, Ted, and Barnie. We regularly exchange pleasantries like: "Roy, you smell like a mackerel that's been left in the sun for three days."

If my brother, K.C., tells me he doesn't want to exchange gifts this Christmas, I know he really doesn't expect my usual Cabela's gift package of "Hot Doe Scent" and stink bait to appear under his tree. He's a guy. He's honest. Women? Not so much.

There are several lady lies that have caused old Joe pain over the years. Here is a partial list for young dudes who, like me, are a little slow.

"I don't want you to buy me anything for our anniversary this year." It's a trap. Buy her a card, flowers, chocolate, and jewelry or you'll sleep alone for a week.

"Be honest. Do you think my butt is getting bigger?" The answer is always: "No." Especially, if you want to see that butt naked anytime soon.

"I don't need a big wedding as long as I marry you." Ha! You will pay for most of the small wedding she has in mind, which includes three hundred guests (two hundred of whom you have never met and, with any luck, will never see again), a twelve-piece band with Grammy nominations, and an open bar featuring only top-shelf liquors because nothing is too good for her hillbilly, beer guzzling relatives or the two hundred strangers you hope to never see again. You will also pay for a wedding dress worth more than your two-year-old pickup truck, and an ice sculpture of Cupid with bow and arrow in hand which will spark a conversation amongst your future in-laws about whether he fires his love arrow from a tree stand or a ground blind.

"I want you to help me plan our wedding—it's your day too." I don't know how they say this with a straight face. Don't even try. There will be no football-shaped groom's cake or servers in Hooters outfits at your wedding reception. Let me repeat: She does not want your opinion. Just agree with whatever she says, but act like you thought about it first.

"You can look all you want; just don't touch any other woman." What she is really saying is: "Eyes to the front mister."

"Tell me the truth (this is always a red flag phrase). Do you think Kate Upton is pretty?" Find a way to avoid answering. If you say "yes," you will pay for it later. Furthermore, you'll be on the receiving end of a lecture, timed to coincide with the final two minutes of the Super Bowl in which your favorite team is tied for the lead and is driving for a score to win the championship for the first time in twenty years. You'll be informed that:

"Kate Upton probably has had work done."

"She's all made up, airbrushed, and Photoshopped."

"You're old enough to be her father." I'm not sure what her point is, but apparently, in the little woman's mind, that's a bad thing.

"I hear she's a real party girl. I'll bet she sleeps with any Tom, Dick, or Harry." Again, I guess that's intended to make me think less of

Kate. I have been married long enough to know better than to respond with: "Have you heard if she sleeps with any Joes?"

Additionally, you can be certain that the next time you casually mention a hunger pang, your sweetheart will suggest: "Why don't you call Kate Upton. Maybe she'll whip you up a casserole."

On the other hand, if you reply that you find Kate repulsive, that her body makes you want to hurl your lunch, your little woman will know you are lying and—guess what—you will pay for it later.

WE'RE LIVING LONGER

When I was growing up in Smalltown, I remember my grandfathers died in their late sixties and my parents being consoled with: "Well, he lived a good, long life."

I think life expectancy for an American male was sixty-seven years.

I guess that should come as no surprise. Their three basic food groups were bacon, sugar, and lard. They drank Budweiser like we drink Poland Spring water, they worked hard at jobs requiring manual labor (they actually made stuff), they raised rug rats by the dozen, and they saw a doctor only if absolutely necessary (i.e. severing an arm or leg with a chainsaw).

Modern science has allowed Americans to live longer. Research shows that we are healthier if we eat better. Consequently, we no longer cook deep fried donuts, French fries, fish sticks, or chicken legs in lard. We use oil from canola beans or extra virgin olives. (Apparently, virgin olives are more healthful than the promiscuous kind.) As a result, we are healthier because these polyunsaturated fats are less likely to clog our arteries and we eat less of our fried favorites because they don't taste anywhere near as good as when we drowned them in animal fat.

We don't eat as much sugar these days either. There are six or seven alternative sweeteners we've concocted in laboratories which contain fewer calories than real sugar and kill us more slowly.

I don't drink as much beer as my grandfathers did and when I do, it is now usually diet beer which has a third the calories, half the alcohol, and a small fraction of the flavor of the Black Label or Narragansett they consumed.

We drink more bottled water because it tastes about the same and provides about the same buzz as diet beer.

When the little woman was diagnosed with high blood pressure, she stopped using salt. There is no longer a salt shaker on the Wright family table and she cooks without sodium products. Our hypertension has improved because we consume less sodium and we've lost weight. It's easier to eat less when food has no flavor.

We eat a lot more lettuce, tomatoes, carrots, and spinach (also known as rabbit food) these days and when the little woman does cook meat, it might be bacon made from turkey, hamburgers made from soy beans, or chicken sausages. I'm sure they are better for me, but they taste like sawdust.

Folks now take prescription drugs to treat their blood pressure, blood sugar, depression, and anxiety. They've got pills to help with sleep (because we don't do enough manual labor to make us tired), and little blue pills so couples can have sex even after they've lost interest. And there's medicine for everything from our thyroids to our hemorrhoids.

These days old folks go to the gym, jog, and watch the boob tube while running on a treadmill. Can you imagine your Grandpa or Pepére doing those things?

Because we eat food that tastes like cardboard, drink more water than beer, jog a lot, and have so little fun, we live, on average, and extra twenty, or so, years longer than our grandparents did . . . and it seems more like forty years.

TODAY'S GADGETS ARE TOO COMPLICATED

Remember when a telephone was a device hooked by wires to a wall and that you could pick up, dial a number, and not only reach the person you called, but actually understand every word they said? I miss those days.

Nowadays, most Americans over the age of six have a "smart phone" that will send and receive text messages and email, allows for George Jetson-like video chats, has a built-in sound system with access to any song ever recorded, functions as a GPS device, and contains a little genie-like woman who can answer your every question and serve your every need (well, almost every need).

Luckily, hardly anyone communicates by telephone call anymore, because these smart phones don't work worth a damn for that. Reception is often so poor that I can only hear about every third or fourth word the little woman says: "So hurry . . . Joe . . . I need you to . . . because . . . breasts . . . and then . . . whipped cream." Then the call is dropped and I don't know whether to stop at the grocery store or the pharmacy on the way home.

Winnie and I bought a new electric kitchen stove about six months ago. We had to take a college course online to learn how to use it.

It used to be that you could just put a pot of venison stew on a burner and turn it to "high" to warm it up fast or "low" to let it simmer. Now there's a special burner for boiling, one for simmering, and one for which you can turn on the middle of the element only, the outside only, or both at once (after completion of the college course).

The oven is even more complicated. You can, once you've hire a computer programmer to set it up, bake with or without convection heating. If you choose to use the convection oven, you simply adjust the baking time suggested by Betty Crocker by a factor of .32791 and add thirteen seconds for every nine percent of the locally forecast relative humidity as reported by the National Weather Service.

A year ago, I purchased a relatively stripped down model of a Dodge pickup truck. It thinks I'm a moron and tells me when to turn, my current gas mileage, how many miles I can drive before I run out of gas, and the pressure in each tire. However, I can't even find the oil filter, let alone change it myself. And to do a basic tune-up, I'd have to get a degree in computer science from M.I.T.

I just read that more than forty percent of new refrigerators must be professionally serviced within four years of purchase. That's because they are too complicated! They self-defrost, dispense water and three sizes of ice cubes from the door, and sound an alarm when you leave the door ajar.

I kept my 1982 avocado-green fridge. It sits in our basement and, after thirty-one years of service-free duty, it still does what I ask of it. The bottom keeps my Bud Light cold, and the top keeps the ice cubes for my Black Velvet and Pepsi frozen. I do have to make my own ice cubes, but that's okay; I may be as stupid as my truck thinks I am, but I remember the recipe for ice. No college degree necessary.

FEED A STARVING MUSICIAN

As I've mentioned, I play in a bluegrass band, Basic Bluegrass, with my buddies, Munzie, Roy, Walt, and Barney. We've played together for years but it seems we make less money with each passing season. Promoters apparently want to pay us what we're worth *without* considering the amount of time, practice, and beer it took for us to reach our special level of pathetic.

Our most common venue is the bluegrass festival, a three- to four-day weekend event which involves a stage show, field picking (jamming with friends and strangers), beer drinking, camping (because you wouldn't want to drive home after all that beer drinking), and overeating—because drinking all that beer builds an appetite.

It's costly to play in a bluegrass band. You must own at least one very expensive stringed instrument because it takes a good guitar, mandolin, fiddle, Dobro, or bass to be heard over a cheap banjo. Let's face it, while banjos rarely sound good, they are always loud.

It is also important that bluegrass musicians own a camper trailer with all the comforts of home and a $30,000 truck to haul it.

So, you see, it takes a lot of festivals making $100 per weekend for the average bluegrass band to break even. I'm not great at math, but I figure we need to play approximately 217 weekends per year to reach that goal.

Free gigs are easy to find. If I had a dollar for every time I've heard: "I just love bluegrass music. Could your band play at our wedding? We can't afford to pay you because my dress costs $1,200 and we are paying $150 to feed each of our 200 guests, not to mention that my flowers will run $1,500, but we'd love to have your band play." The final plea is usually, "It doesn't pay anything, but it will be great exposure for you." Yes, more unpaid gigs is just what we need to make money.

Nursing homes are common spots to play free gigs. We once performed at the Pine Hill Nursing Home and Assisted Living Center. We played right in the dining hall. Next to Walt, our banjo player, was a giant bowl of pretzels.

Walt loves pretzels, and while he complained that these particular twisted snacks were stale and lacked salt, he munched on a handful after each song.

By the time we finished, Walt had eaten the entire bowl and felt a bit guilty. He apologized to Gladys, a resident at Pine Hill, but she said: "That's okay. Mabel and I were done with those pretzels anyway. They've put us on a gluten-free diet, so we just suck the chocolate off 'em and put 'em back in the bowl."

TIME FLIES

When I was a kid, we told "Little Moron" jokes. I suppose these day, they'd be considered insensitive, or politically incorrect, but, to be honest, I'm not even sure of the definition of moron.

Our Little Moron jokes were lame, but hilarious to an eight-year-old. For example: Why did the Little Moron close his eyes when he opened the refrigerator? He didn't want to see the salad dressing.

I told you that joke so I could tell you this: Why did the Little Moron throw his watch out the window? He wanted to see time fly.

Growing up in Smalltown, I remember my Pepére saying that each year seemed to go by faster and faster as he grew older. I heard Mr. Whitney at the barber shop say the same thing and I recall thinking how ridiculous such an idea seemed. At five, it seemed like it took forever before I was old enough to attend kindergarten. At eleven, it seemed like I'd never turn twelve so that I could have my first real rifle—a J.C. Higgins .22 caliber. I needed that rifle to pay back the hundreds of red squirrels that taunted me and my cousin, Mick, every time we hunted the woods behind our home with lame BB guns.

At fifteen, I got my driver's learning permit and it seemed like years until I turned sixteen and was able to get my license. I'm not sure why I was in such a hurry. It didn't change my love life in the way I expected.

When I was eighteen, I couldn't wait to be twenty-one so I could buy my own Pabst Blue Ribbon instead of depending on my older brother for that. Turned out I didn't have to wait those three long years. Before I turned nineteen, the State, in its wisdom, lowered the drinking age to eighteen. Finally, I could go to bars and clubs and charm the pants off eighteen-year-old girls. That didn't work out so well either.

So, time dragged on until my mid-twenties when I married Winnie and soon Jake and Maggie were born. Suddenly, it seemed like the hands on the clock started spinning at hyperspeed.

It's over forty years since John Travolta was doing the Hustle in *Saturday Night Fever*. I've always had two left feet and I never owned one of those tight polyester leisure suits that were so popular back then, but Travolta and I do have something in common. We are both about forty pounds heavier than we were in the seventies. Time flies.

My son, Jake, will turn forty next week. It seems like yesterday that he was a baby and I was changing his dirty diapers, cleaning spit-up from his shirt (and mine) and pushing him around in a stroller. It's scary to think about how quickly those forty years have passed and that, in another forty years, he'll either be doing the same stuff for me or I'll be pushing up daisies. Time flies—whether or not you're having fun.

BAGGING A BUCK CAN BE KIND OF A DRAG

I really enjoy my game cameras. I have three of them now and hang them from trees along well-known deer runs on Buck Mountain near the Smalltown Boys' Camp north of home.

Last fall, my brother, K.C., his son, Eli, and I were some excited by the pre-deer season photos captured on the cameras. I got shots of several nice whitetails, but there was one image that made our hearts beat faster than my chubby cousin Ralphie's at the All You Can Eat Buffet down at the China Palace. This deer was a big eight pointer, so fat we called him "the pig." He'd apparently helped himself to apples and acorns like it was his job.

Following a week at camp—that's hours of hunting, poker, over-eating and beer guzzling—we'd seen a few deer, but not "the pig," which by now had morphed into the "The Giant Pig."

I was hunting with my nephew when we heard a gunshot that kinda sounded like it came from his father's direction. But it also sounded like it came from miles away, so we paid little attention and finished our Butterfinger and Snickers power snacks.

A half hour later, Eli checked his iPhone for messages. There were twelve new texts, all from K.C., telling us he'd bagged "The Giant Pig" and could use some help.

Needless to say, Eli and I hustled—as fast as my sixty-two-year-old body can hustle—to my brother's aid. Meanwhile, our buddy, Roy, heard the shot, but then thought about the dragging to follow and quickly ran back to camp.

After thirty minutes of admiring the massive buck, field dressing and photo taking, it was time to drag him to the cabin where our

Dad, who was now aware of K.C.'s trophy, was anxiously awaiting our arrival.

Eli held all three rifles as K.C. and I each grabbed a side of the big rack and gave it a tug to haul the big boy out of the little gulley where he had come to his final resting place. "The Giant Pig" mocked us and hardly budged.

K.C. looked at his much older brother, and politely suggested it might make more sense for me to carry the guns and for my nephew to replace me as a deer dragger.

I was too relieved to take insult so I took the rifles from Eli. The drag out of the gulley was slow but, luckily, short. The rest of the haul was down the steep, snow-covered mountainside logging road to camp.

As the senior member of our hunting party, I diligently led the way, at least for a while. Gravity was working in favor of the younger draggers and soon my brother said to me: "I hate to add insult to injury, bro, but could you get your fat ass out of the way so we don't run you over?"

For someone who hates to insult me, K.C. sure is good at it.

An hour and a half later, we got back to the camp where "Ol' Dad" was pacing the floor. Dad doesn't pace as fast as he once did. He's suffered some nerve damage to his legs which has slowed him down a bit.

My brother was the first to notice that the cabin was as neat as a pin; the floors swept, the beds made, the dishes done.

"What got into you Dad?" he asked.

Dad looked a little sheepish and explained. "Old habits. After you called, I got so excited I put on my draggin' boots, my hunting pants, and my wool jacket and then said to myself: "Damn, I forgot. I can hardly walk."

"So, I was so nerved up, I cleaned the camp, instead."

126

We made some more memories that day. My younger brother made me proud—again. Not only did he put his deer hunting skills to good use and bag a trophy buck, he also showed me a talent I didn't know he possessed. As we neared the end of the drag, he stopped, looked up at the nearly clear sky, tugged at his beard, took off his hat, pointed to a small cluster of clouds and made a very accurate forecast: "I think there's a good chance it'll get drunk out tonight."

ANNOYING FACEBOOK FRIENDS

Two years ago, my daughter, Maggie, convinced me I should be on Facebook. "It'll help you stay connected with all your friends," she explained. "It's fun."

Now, somehow, I have 367 Facebook "friends." Shoot, I can't think of thirty-six people I actually like, so, how do I have 367 "friends" on a social media site?

I hate to admit it, but I do look at Facebook every day. It's like a car wreck. I know I shouldn't look at it, but I can't help myself.

There are many people on Facebook that annoy the bejeebers out of me. I've developed fictitious characters to represent some of these folks and have given them some ever-so-clever names. *Miss Anita Life* gives you a breathless moment-to-moment account of her seemingly uneventful existence; *Mr. I.M. Fabulous* feels the need to share how wonderful his life is; and *Mrs. Y. Mee* wants to share all the painful, unfair events that collectively define her miserable existence here on Earth.

I have ranked these three groups based on just how much each grates at my nerves and have saved the worst for last.

First of all, *Anita Life*, I don't need to know every time you plug in a Crock Pot of chili. It's *not* newsworthy and I don't care. Furthermore, I don't need to see ten new recipes daily for bacon-wrapped hot dogs, chocolate-covered cheesecake, or crème-filled, deep fried, chocolate-covered Twinkies with ice cream and whipped topping. I'm fat enough, and besides, I have a running tab at all the best restaurants in Smalltown. And *no*, I don't want to play Farmville or Candy Crush with you.

As for you, *Mr. Fabulous,* I know you want me (and the rest of the world) to know how wonderful your life is, but please keep it to yourself. You're not making me feel any better about mine.

I don't need to know that you have the "most wonderful wife in the world." Don't tell me; tell her—to her face. Let's be honest, the only reason to share that crap on the internet is to make *you* look wonderful to the world. *Oh, isn't he sweet?* My guess is that if you feel the need to tell the world how wonderful your marriage is, it probably isn't.

And please, *Mr. Fabulous,* don't ask me to: "Share if you have a daughter who's beautiful and wonderful." I do, and she knows I feel that way because I tell her so—in person. My friends on Facebook, who know Maggie, know it too. So if you haven't spoken to your little girl since she ran off with the carnival worker, don't try to make up with her on social media, give her a call or a visit.

And finally, *Mrs. Y. Mee,* I don't need to share your pain on Facebook. I'm sorry you are always feeling poorly, but please don't feel the need to share every time you cough, sneeze, or have the runs. Tell your doctor. I don't need to know.

And, for crying out loud, don't air your dirty laundry for the entire world to see. I'm sure that, after that third tequila shot, it seems like the perfect time to even the score with your ex-husband for doing you wrong, but you really should avoid the Patrón post. I don't care that Ralphie cheated on you with your best friend, Molly, or that he brought home a virus and shared it with you. That crap doesn't belong on social media. That's not the way to get even with Ralphie. You need to grow up and handle your personal problems privately and with dignity. Go torch his new Camaro or sleep with his brother, but don't litter the worldwide web with your problems. Follow my example and reserve Facebook for really important things—such as liking every picture of my adorable granddaughter and following my detailed play-by-play analysis of the Patriots game I'm watching on TV.

I JUST WANT TO BUY THIS BAG OF WASHERS

Last summer, the little woman mentioned the lawn mower was pushing harder than usual. She requested my help in her usual seemingly polite way.

"You might want to take a look at the lawn mower when you get a chance," she said.

I've lived with Winnie long enough to know that sweetness translates to: "Look at the lawn mower right now or you'll be pushing it yourself, you lazy old bastard."

So, I tell her I'll get to it when I get to it, and then quickly jump up off the couch to check the Lawn Boy. It seems she has pushed it so many miles over the years that she has worn out the washers that allow the wheels to turn smoothly.

I decided to run down to Small-Mart and pick up some washers. Otherwise, it would take her longer to mow, cost me more money in gasoline, and force me to listen to that annoying engine whine for a longer stretch. Three hours is long enough; it already nearly drowns out an entire Red Sox game. Plus, I'm afraid I'll hear about the need for a riding mower; like we need one of those. She's mowing only two acres.

Anyway, I told you all that just to tell you it isn't easy to buy a bag of washers these days.

Luckily, the emergency occurred during the seventh inning stretch, so I figured I could run across town, grab four washers, and get back for the ninth inning. Not as easy as it seemed.

First, it took me a while to find a decent parking spot. It seems like everyone is lazy and wants to park close to the store entrance. I

131

drove around and around for ten minutes before I could find a spot within *my* walking distance.

Then it took me time to find the washers I needed. There is no hardware section at Small-Mart. It turns out they wedge the washers in between toilet parts and waste baskets. I don't get it. Maybe it's alphabetical.

The worst part, though, occurred at the checkout counter. After waiting behind three other customers, (I always get in line behind the chatty woman with three separate orders and needs a price check on each of item), I finally reached the cashier, Edith.

Edith rang up the washers and I handed her a dollar bill.

"Do you have a Small-Mart customer loyalty card?" she asked.

"No," I replied.

"Your address please?"

"I just want to buy these washers, Edith. I'm not looking for a pen pal."

"I was just gonna look to see if you have a Small-Mart Customer Loyalty Card and didn't know it," Edith said. "You could save one percent on your purchase."

"It's 69 cents. I'd save less than a penny," I said. "I told you I don't have the card."

"Would you like to apply for one? It takes only ten minutes and you could save on this and future purchases," Edith explained.

"No dammit. Just give me my washers and 31 cents and I'll be on my way," I pleaded.

"All right sir, your zip code?"

"My zip code? Why in the world do you need that?"

"It helps the company track where our customers come from. The computer won't let me cash you out without it."

"I live in Smalltown. It's the same zip as this store. Please hurry."

"I'll need your email address."

"What the . . . "

"In case there's a recall on your purchase. The company wants to be able to let you know," Edith explained.

"Forget it. Keep your damned washers. I'll go to Fred's like I should have to begin with."

And that's exactly what I did. I walked into Fred's Hardware, went straight to the right section, picked up four loose washers, and took them over to Cheryl, my next door neighbor, at the cash register.

"Hi Joe, zip code please," she said.

BABIES ARE BIG BUSINESS THESE DAYS

Things surely have changed since the little woman and I raised our kids.

Jake and Maggie are now raising young ones of their own and it is gratifying to see them doing such a fine job. Grandchildren are wonderful. As the saying goes: "Grandchildren are God's reward to us for not strangling our children when they were teenagers."

Still, I can't help but notice how much more careful about child rearing our kids are compared to when we were bringing them up. They've got complicated gadgets and special foods we never dreamed and they (or we) pay dearly for all of it.

It makes me wonder if the pediatricians all own stock in stores like Babies-B-Us or Buy Baby Buy Buy Buy!

Babies these days never have a private moment. Thanks to modern technology, they are watched at all times, even in the crib. Maggie and her husband, Roscoe, have a digital, high-def camera with Dolby surround sound to monitor little Gracie's every move. She can't pick her nose or burp without her parents knowing about it. It's kind of creepy to me, like something from a George Orwell novel. "Big Mother" is always watching.

Swaddling is a new phenomenon. For those of you who are my age and don't have grandkids, a swaddle is a blanket-like contraption that has Velcro on it so that the baby can be tightly wrapped with arms confined to her sides. It's a baby straightjacket! It's supposed to make Gracie more comfortable as she sleeps but I don't think so. Otherwise, she wouldn't try so hard to escape, as she always does. She's a little Houdini.

I'd suggest wrapping Maggie tightly in duct tape just before bedtime to see how she likes that, except that I'd like more grandchildren someday.

Winnie and I bought a "changing table" for Jake and Jenna before Hanson was born. It's a special table for diaper changing. I don't see the need for it. In our day, we'd just drop the wet baby on the couch and change the diaper.

These days, every kid has to ride in a protective car seat until they are practically in junior high school. Gone are the days when little Jake sat on my lap and helped me drive through town while his baby sister lay on a blanket in the passenger seat of my F-150.

I remember pushing Maggie around in a three dollar stroller with wheels that seemed to turn in every direction except the one in which I was trying to travel.

When she asked if we could buy the Baby Rider Cruisomatic Stroller System for Gracie, I said: "Of course. Anything for our baby granddaughter."

Little did I know the Baby Rider costs more, by about $300, than my first car. Not that it would have mattered.

Hanson and Sumner drink milk like it is going out of style. It must be organic milk because Dr. Rugratter says so. They also eat organically grown carrot and banana smoothies. I guess their folks figure feeding the boys healthy food for the first few years will provide a good base for all those Whopper Bacon Cheeseburgers, French fries, and chocolate milk shakes they'll consume later.

MOST TV INFOMERCIALS ARE A SCAM

It seems like those thirty-minute commercials they run on television are always aired at times when only people without a job or social life are watching. It's like the marketing folks for companies that sell weight loss products and male enhancement pills say: "Hey, it's four a.m. on a Sunday. Let's sell our stuff to the losers who are awake because they couldn't find a date on Saturday night."

By the way, those male enhancement pills don't work. I don't know that from personal experience, honest. But someone, let's say my buddy, Walt, told me. I think these companies make money because they know I—I mean guys like Walt—won't take advantage of their "satisfaction guaranteed or your money back" policy. Besides, I think Walt was plenty satisfied, it was the little woman who didn't get her money's worth.

I'm not saying that all products sold through infomercials are a scam. I've gotten fair use out of my Whacky Waffle Machine. I love those little syrup-drenched batter cakes and the Whacky Waffle makes it easy to enjoy them three or four times a week. I especially enjoy my waffles since I also ordered the Ice Cream Factory from the nice lady in the TV who included two Whip Zip whipped cream attachments for free (plus $20 additional shipping and handling).

Sure, I love waffles. But waffles with ice cream *and* whipped topping are to die for (and I likely *will* die sooner than I would otherwise for enjoying too many cream laden waffles), but I'll die fat, dumb, and happy with a whipped cream moustache.

I'm thinking there may be a conspiracy between the marketers of machines like Whacky Waffle and Whip Zip and the many purveyors of fitness, weight loss, and exercise products promising to whip us back into shape.

Last week, I watched a half-hour ad for a video called *Buns of Steel.* Seriously? When it comes to booty, I prefer something with a little jiggle to something I can pound nails with. I watched the entire ad though. It was either tune in to those three very fit ladies dancing to "Honky Tonk Bedonkedonk" or an Oprah rerun.

My brother, K.C., once fell for the infomercial for the Ab Glider, which promised "six-pack abs in five minutes a day." I really doubted that the machine was going to work out for my little brother because I once watched him drink five six-packs in one day. I think he was the inspiration for the modern day thirty-pack.

One of the other selling points for the Ab Glider was its compact design. It folds up and easily fits under the bed which, I'm quite sure, is where K.C.'s machine has spent all of the past six months.

My cousin, Elsie, is a big girl and a sucker for a TV promise. She wants to lose eighty pounds and Christie Brinkley convinced her that they'll be nearly identical if Elsie sends her a check for $1,200 for the amazing EZ Slider. She sent the money.

I noticed just last week that Elsie had an ad in *The Smalltown News* for a slightly used Stair Climber, a Belly Blaster, three *Flabmaster* CDs, and four Suzanne Somers workout videos. Her ad read: "$80 takes the whole lot."

I wonder what she will get for the EZ Slider next month?

A DAY AT THE DOCTOR'S OFFICE

Last month I had a bellyache on a Saturday, so I called Dr. Braley's office only to be greeted by the recorded voice of Bernice, his receptionist for the past thirty-five years or so.

Bernice's voice told me if I was feeling poorly and didn't think I could wait until Monday, I should drive to the Quick Care Clinic in St. Jamesboro.

Seeing as how I was throwing up beans, hot dogs, jalapeño peppers, Slim Jims, deer liver, and pickled eggs, I figured I should do just that and have someone smarter than me figure out why I'd taken sick.

The receptionist at the clinic, Tiffany, looked to be about thirteen, but she must have been at least sixteen because I believe that is the minimum legal age for working in a position where your decisions could determine who lives or dies.

I told Tiffany I felt really ill and she immediately added: "I can tell, you look really bad, just awful." She quickly handed me twenty-seven pages of paperwork to complete before someone could see me and figure out why I looked so terrible.

"What's all this?" I asked.

She tried to explain. "This one is to tell us who we can like share your information with."

"I don't care who knows I've been upchucking animal parts. Hell, you can post pictures of me puking on *Instagram* for all I care."

There were three pages to tell about every ailment ever suffered by a member of my family.

"Jumpin' Jeepers Tiffany, my Uncle Herbert had a rash on his butt fifty years ago after courting Jolene Henderson in a poison ivy patch. Do you need that on this paper?"

"Sure, Mr. Wright, that goes under dermatology."

I seemingly filled out paperwork for three hours. The Quick Care Clinic now knows way more about me and my family than Winnie does.

Finally, an older woman—I'm guess maybe thirty—called my name.

"Thank you, Doctor. I don't feel well."

"Yes, you look awful," she said, quickly confirming Tiffany's assessment. "I'm not the doctor. I'm Jody and I'll be getting some information for Dr. Green."

Over the next few hours, Jody and her friends ran my body through the alphabet soup of health care tests. I think I had an MRI, MRA, EKG, RBI and an ERA. She filled fourteen vials with my blood and made me pee into a plastic cup.

Eight hours after I arrived at the Quick Care Clinic, Dr. Green blew through my exam room like a monkey on amphetamines. He bounced around the room, rifled through test results, glanced at me, gave me a sad face, and spoke to Jody almost faster than I could hear.

"I agree. Let's keep him at least four more hours," and left the room without ever uttering a syllable to me. "He looks awful."

"I feel fine now," I protested. "I've been here all day. I'm over my sickness."

Jody put her hands on her hips, stomped her foot, and told me where I stood. "I'm sorry Mr. Wright. We can't let you leave now. You still look just awful."

I stayed at the clinic for four more hours before they decided my prognosis was poor. They gave up on curing me from looking awful and sent me home to people who have gotten used to this face.

E.M.S. FOR P.M.S.

You don't have to be from a big town to know about EMS—you know, Emergency Medical Services. That's when you dial 9-1-1 because you have a big problem and you need help. Even the Smalltown Fire Department will respond with an ambulance to a 9-1-1 call when that chest pain you've endured for three weeks suddenly becomes an emergency because it is the Friday before deer season and you don't want to head north to deer camp if you are on the verge of a heart attack. (You were sure the pain would go away on its own by now.)

But this article is about the need for a different kind of E.M.S.—the Estrogen Management System.

God played a joke on Mankind. He subjected women to PMS, a monthly event that for many women involve belly cramps, headaches, and violent mood swings. Winnie always suffered greatly during her monthly cycle.

To make things worse, he created partners for many women who are clueless when it comes to dealing with it. Unfortunately for Winnie, I was worse than most men and never got a handle on it.

Let me tell you a story to illustrate.

Several years ago, Winnie was sitting on the La-Z-Boy crying when I got home from work.

"What's wrong?" I asked, sensitive husband that I am.

"Your sister hates me."

"What makes you say that?"

"Well . . . sniff, sniff . . . today I called her to see if she wanted to go to the Presidents' Day sale at J.C. Penney and she said: 'No, thank you.'"

More tears and sobbing.

"Well, dear, Kelly did fall off the chair lift and break both legs just two weeks ago. It's probably hard for her to shop in a wheelchair," I reassured her.

"Oh sure, take her side. She's family. I'm just your stupid wife."

"No darling," I explained. "I'm not taking her side and you *are* my wife which is just as important as family."

"Oh, but I *am* stupid, huh? I see you're not denying that."

"No, you're not my stupid wife. You're just my plain old wife."

"Great! So now I'm plain and I'm old."

I soldiered on.

"Kelly doesn't hate you. She loves you and so do I."

Now she hugs me and says she's sorry.

"I don't know what's wrong with me. I get so moody sometimes."

"I know dear," I said and then once again fell into the trap. "It's just that time of the month again."

Whoops!

"Oh sure, blame it on that again. It's always *that* when we fight. It's never your fault, Mr. $@&$%# Perfect."

Now her eyes are bulging and I swear I see little flames shooting from her nostrils.

"I think I'll just go to bed," I say. "I've had a rough day."

"Oh sure, just go to bed with dishes in the sink and a mess to pick up. You think my day was a walk in the park? Let me tell you about my day . . ."

A few years before menopause I finally learned a few things. Well, mostly just to shut up and never, ever blame something on "that time of the month." But there are few other lessons I'd like to share and hopefully help you younger guys who may be struggling.

Average Joe's Estrogen Management System

Rule #1: Do *not* pretend to know what she's going through.

"You don't know what it's like. You're not a woman. You don't have to go through this every damned month."

It is hard to argue with the first two sentences. You're *not* a woman. Never suggest that you *do* go through it every month. It'll only make the pain greater.

Rule #2: Do *not* offer her Pamprin or Midol.

"Oh sure, you think a little pill will solve all my problems. You just want me to get rid of the cramps so I won't be so grouchy. Well, maybe, Mister, if you'd help me with the kids and the housework, I wouldn't feel so miserable."

You may find, however, two Pamprin tablets washed down with a Bud Light helps ease your own pain. Consult your doctor.

Rule #3: Do *not* videotape her irrational behavior.

Sure, she may be temporarily crazy, but documenting it is *never, ever* a good idea.

Rule #4: Do *not* suggest mood elevating drugs.

I know the TV ads for products like Concerta make it sound like these chemicals will change her mood from heavy metal head-banging music to soothing violins and cellos but, trust me, you'd rather listen to ten hours of banjos and bagpipes than to endure her verbal response caused by your suggestion that she should try some "crazy pills." Of course, you might make out better if you didn't use the words "crazy pills" as a suggested remedy.

Rule #5: Hang in there buddy . . . this will end.

And then there's menopause.

ABOUT THE AUTHOR

Brian Daniels is an avid outdoorsman, blogger, novelist, musician and songwriter. His first novel, *Luke's Dream,* was released in January, 2011. His humorous commentary, *Thoughts of an Average Joe* by Joe Wright ("Thoughts of an Average Brian" just doesn't have the same ring), has been featured in such publications as *The Huffington Post* and the *Bangor Daily News*. His second book, *Thoughts of an Average Joe,* was released in April, 2014. Brian was born and raised in Vermont's "Northeast Kingdom." His childhood hometown, Lyndonville, serves as inspiration for Average Joe's "Smalltown." Brian is a retired U.S. Naval officer. From 1984 to 2014, he practiced optometry in Brunswick, Maine where he lives with his wife, Laurene.